Journeys and Ends

A Short Story Collection

Dale T. Phillips

ISBN: 9798262741304

The Tree of Sorrows was first published in *Plot*, Summer 1996
The Great Snipe Hunt was first published in *New Myths*,
March 2010
Yesterday and Today was first published in *Space and Time*, Summer
1996, and later in *Atomjack*, Issue #87
God Save the Queen was first published in *Kasma*, March 2010
Night of the Annoying Dead was first published in *Flashes in the
Dark*, December, 2010

Try these other works by Dale T. Phillips

Shadow of the Wendigo (Supernatural Thriller)
Neptune City (Mystery)
Locust Time (Suspense)
Desert Heat (Crime/Mystery)

The Zack Taylor Mystery Series

A Great Reckoning
A Darkened Room

A Sharp Medicine
A Certain Slant of Light
A Shadow on the Wall
A Fall From Grace
A Memory of Grief

Story Collections

The Big Book of Genre Stories (Different Genres)
Crime Time (Mystery/Crime)
Halls of Fear (Horror)
Journeys and Ends (Magic Realism, End of the World)
All the Crooked Paths (Mystery/Crime)
All the Fables and Fantasies (Fantasy)
Jumble Sale (Different Genres)

Non-fiction Career Help

How to be a Successful Indie Writer
87 Ways to Sell More Books
How to Conquer Excuses and Just Write
How to Win
How to Improve Your Interviewing Skills

Sign up for my newsletter to get special offers
http://www.daletphillips.com

Dedication

For Jesse, who saw many strange things, and who made a difference.

Dale T. Phillips

CONTENTS

ROADSIDE ATTRACTION

Guy had been on the road for days, and felt crumbled around the edges. Running away wasn't easy, because at some point, you had to stop, and the horrors that you were running from had time to catch up. So you pushed yourself far beyond the limits of any sane person, off into some other world, where sights and sounds and smells could fool you. Your mind played tricks, and you were just too tired to figure it out.

Driving too far for too long can be deadly, and Guy desperately needed to stop and rest. He'd reached the end of his endurance, and could not go much further, but there was nothing available. He was in the desert, he was aware of that much, but wasn't even sure which state. He had, however, recently spotted a saguaro cactus, and thought he'd remembered reading somewhere that they only grow in Arizona. Okay then. Maybe he'd go to the Grand Canyon, and see if all that big empty could match what was inside him. Or maybe he'd check out Meteor Crater, and look at the monstrous hole blasted into the earth from some wayward space debris, and think of how fate had done something similar to him.

But right now, Guy needed sleep more than anything. A sane person, however, does not sleep in their car under the hot desert sun. So he drove on, looking for solace.

And then he saw the sign:

Roadside Attraction
Jerome's Killer Snake Farm & Mr. K's Diner
Gas, GUNS, Cold Drinks, Curios

Guy smiled at the combination of offerings. Something for the whole family. Family. He shut off that tap before more flowed, and checked his gas gauge. Less than a quarter of a tank, so he'd have to stop. Despite his pain, he had no wish to be stranded, foolishly to die under a withering, pitiless sun.

In the flat plain of the desert, Guy saw the place for miles before he reached it. Like a mirage, it seemed to waver in the distance, forever pulling away just out of reach. But he finally neared the cluster of buildings, and turned his wheels from the droning safety of the highway to the hard-baked dirt of the scorched parking lot.

The complex was a jumble of different worlds. On one side was a shabby-but-still-functioning filling station, with dusty windows, broken, peeling signs, and ancient gas pumps. Various pieces of rusted auto parts lay scattered, baking in the sun like misshapen metal cookies. A hand-lettered sign with an arrow pointed the way to the Killer Snake Farm. Another crude sign proclaimed Curios, and pointed to a small adjoining shack.

Across the lot was a small diner, looking immaculately sleek and new, and completely out of place. The black-and-chrome finish made it appear as if it had been dropped from space, amidst the squalor of the other buildings.

Guy thought that a cool, clean place would be wonderful about now, and he parked and headed for the diner, which looked as if it would be air-conditioned. The heat was intense when he left the cocoon of his car, and Guy's throat was so dry, he couldn't even work up enough saliva to swallow. The air was as thick and hot as an animal's breath, and Guy's fatigue made the walk unbearable. He moved slowly, almost like he was swimming through the thick air, and it seemed to take a while to reach the diner door. In the stillness, he heard music coming from inside. Old music, some forgotten tune of a long time before.

The metal door handle burned Guy's hand when he gripped it, and he pulled back in alarm. He realized it had absorbed too much heat from the sun, so he took out a handkerchief, and used it as protection while he pulled the door open.

A wave of cool air washed over Guy from the inside of the diner, and he swayed in grateful thanks. The door hissed shut behind him, as if sealing him inside the coolness. He looked around.

Two girls in white dresses sat at a table by themselves. They were young, about twelve, just like...

"Hello," Guy called out, shutting out the completion of the thought. He walked to the counter and called out again. The music ended, and there was a stillness.

Guy forced himself to look at the girls. Identical twins. Their hair was nightshade black, contrasting with the frilly white party dresses they wore. The ribbon in each girls' hair was a different color, though, red for one and green for the other. They looked at him, and

7

one put her hand to her mouth and whispered something, which made the other one giggle. Guy tried to smile, although it felt as if he had broken glass in his thoughts.

"Anybody else around?" His voice came out strained and harsh. He tried clearing his throat. They did not speak to him, but looked like they were now playing a game of some sort with each other. Guy shrugged and sat on a stool at the counter. Everything was new, gleaming in polished perfection, and Guy marveled. He'd never seen anyplace this clean, let alone a diner. It looked as if they never served food here. In fact, Guy saw no menus.

"Ah, a customer."

Guy looked up at the voice, and saw an older, sharp-faced, well-dressed man in a crisply tailored suit and tie addressing him from behind the counter. The man must have just come through the swinging doors leading to the kitchen, but they were not moving. Guy blinked, his eyes gritty.

"Hi there."

"And what can I do for you?" The man's voice was smooth, like something sliding over oily rocks.

"How about a glass of water to start?" Guy rasped.

"The essence of life. Yes, indeed." The man reached under the counter and came up with a filled glass of water. It even had ice, and condensation had beaded on the outside of the glass. Guy was puzzled as to how or why it had been kept like that, but the vision of the cool water made him dizzy with anticipation. The man set it on the counter. Guy picked it up and swallowed it in three long gulps. The man watched him.

"Would you like some more?"

"Yes, please."

The man reached under the counter again, and came up with another filled glass like the first. Guy took longer to finish this one, wondering in the back of his mind why the man hadn't just refilled his glass.

The man looked at him with an intense gaze. "Is there anything else I can do for you this day?"

Guy smiled. "I don't suppose you've got a room for rent, where I could catch a nap."

The man shook his head. "No, I'm afraid the closest motel is one hundred and sixteen miles of hot desert road that way. There are some needs even we cannot fill."

Guy nodded. "How about some lunch, then?"

The man cocked his head. "You want something to eat?"

"Well, yeah. Isn't that why people come in?"

The man almost smiled. "People come here for many things."

"Ah, yes," said Guy. "Snakes, curios, and guns. But you do have food as well, don't you?"

"Oh, yes, we have food."

"Do you have a menu?"

The man looked around, as if suddenly surprised by the lack of menus, and the request for such a thing. "Why don't you tell me what you want, and I'll see if I can get it for you."

"Okay, how about a cheeseburger and fries, with a large root beer on the side?"

The man smiled and made an almost imperceptible bow. "Coming right up."

"What about the girls there? They yours?"

"Sir?" The man looked puzzled.

Guy turned to look as he gestured. "The two girls--" but there was no one else in the room. He looked back at the man. "There were twin girls in white dresses sitting at that table."

The man cocked his head. "If you say so, sir."

Guy was confused.

The man opened his hands in a gesture, as if he could not determine how to proceed. "Shall I get your food, sir?"

"Sure, whatever."

Guy got up to use the restroom, walking to the side hallway. Like other diners, this one had pictures of the owner with other people, framed photos of people that one might assume were some sort of celebrity. But Guy recognized none of the people in the photographs, though they were posing as if they were somebody famous. The framed photos were off, somehow, a trifle unsettling, as though there was something the camera was not showing in the scene. One looked to be at a funeral. Another had people with a car in the background, but unlike any car Guy had seen. He made a mental note to ask the owner about it.

In the restroom, Guy emptied his bladder and washed his hands, and then his face, splashing cool water on the back of his neck. He felt more awake and less gritty. He noticed a sign, one of those admonishing the employees. But the wording was different on this one.

Employees are strongly encouraged to wash themselves before returning to work

Underneath was lettering in some other language, but Guy could not recognize it. The font was strange, and some of the letters didn't look like letters at all.

Guy shook his head, and went for something to dry his hands. The dispenser was one of those old-fashioned, chrome, toaster-like wall devices that had a cloth towel suspended as a hanging loop. You were supposed to grab a little and pull down on one side, which made the other side get pulled up into the dispenser. Guy hadn't seen one of these in years, probably because they didn't seem very sanitary, if used a lot. At least this one seemed spotless and fresh.

Shaking his head, Guy walked back out to the main room. He stopped to catch his breath. The girls were back at the table, whispering to one another. He wondered if something was happening to his mind, and rationality kicked in to suggest to him that they might have simply been using the other restroom, which is why the man at the counter hadn't seen them. It was damned odd, though, Guy thought. He was curious enough to want to check it out, despite the warning bells going off in his head.

"Hello, young ladies," Guy said, trying to appear casual. On his face, he'd pasted what he hoped might resemble a friendly smile.

They looked at him, eyes wide.

"Where's your folks? Your Mom or Dad?"

The girls whispered to each other, and then turned to address Guy. The one with the green ribbon spoke in solemn tones. "We can't be with them anymore."

"Oh." Guy wondered. He didn't want to press further, afraid of what might break out.

"Does the man behind the counter know you're here?"

The one with the red ribbon now took a turn speaking. "He doesn't yet, but he will."

"I see," Guy said, but he was more puzzled than before.

"Do you want to play a game?" The girl with the green ribbon addressed him.

11

"What kind of game?"

"We call it Memaginary," said the twin with the red ribbon. " You bring up the memory of the most terrible thing that's ever happened to you, and then try to imagine something worse."

Guy's eyes suddenly burned with tears. He stumbled backward, aghast. The girls were staring at him, as if they had bets on what he would do. He couldn't think straight, he decided, he was too fatigued. Guy spun away from them, and from his own thoughts, and went back to his counter stool.

The man was just setting a plate in place. "Here you go. Just what the doctor ordered."

Guy plucked at the man's sleeve. The fabric was warm, smooth, and shiny. "The girls there. They said you didn't know they were there yet, but you would.?"

"Ah. I see. Yes, those two do cause a bit of trouble from time to time."

"Where are their parents? They said they couldn't be with them anymore."

"Well... it's complicated."

"How so?"

"Don't you worry about it sir. I'll see that they don't bother you again."

"It's just--" Guy was looking for the right thing to say.

"You'd better eat. Your meat's getting cold."

Guy looked down at the plate. There was a burger, complete inside the most perfect bun Guy had ever seen. Each half of the bun had no irregular edges, but looked as if it had been cut and shaped with a jeweler's precision. There were exactly two dozen french fries on the plate, all carbon copies of each other, all neatly arranged, like a perfect little pile of cordwood.

"Looks nice," said Guy.

"Looks can be deceiving," said the man, setting an old-fashioned glass on the counter, filled to the brim with bubbly soda, and three perfect ice cubes. Guy, still thirsty, took a sip.

"That's really good." He took a larger swallow. "Amazing. Not like the stuff you get in supermarkets."

"No indeed," the man replied.

Guy took a bite from the burger, and a wonderful taste sensation flooded his mouth. It was probably the best burger he'd ever tried. It needed no condiments, and had subtle, almost spicy flavors underneath. He tried one of the french fries, and they were incredibly delicious. Guy looked at the man.

"The food is excellent."

The man made a slight bow. "I thank you for saying so."

"You must be Mr. K."

"I am known by that name."

"With food this good, you could make a fortune closer to a city, instead of way out here."

"Ah, but what if I have no need to make my fortune? And cities are no place to live."

"I guess you're right," said Guy, chewing another mouthful.

"So what brings you all the way out here?"

Guy stopped chewing. He couldn't say what was in his mind: Running away, so I don't have to face what happened. Getting by in a sort of living death, pushing ever forward, with no looks back over your shoulder.

"You know," said Guy. "Seeing the sights."

"Sights? There aren't any sights out here that you'd want to see."

"But I'm going to them. You know, further on." Even to himself, Guy knew it was weak.

"Well, I wish you luck in finding whatever it is you're looking for."

"Thanks," Guy said, then finished the last of his meal.

"Will there be anything else, sir?"

"I guess not. What's the damages?"

"Pretty severe, I would guess."

Guy winced. "No, I mean what do I owe you?"

The man spread his hands in an expansive gesture. "Special today. No charge for the weary traveler."

Guy frowned. "No, come on, really. That was the best burger I've ever had."

"Your money is no good here today, sir."

"Well, that's a hell of a thing."

"To be sure."

"You do this a lot? Give away free meals?"

"Only to select customers."

"Thank you, then."

"You take care, out on that road, sir. Anything can happen."

"Sure thing. Hey, there's a car in one of your photos on the wall, but what kind is it? I don't recognize it."

"Foreign model," said the man.

Guy turned to see if the girls were there, and they were. Guy turned back to the man, but he was already gone. Guy blinked in surprise. No one would believe him if he told them about this place. Not that there was anyone to tell, now. As Guy was walking out, he noticed that there was no cash register, either. Maybe the man had it out back, where he could keep an eye on it. Or maybe there wasn't one at all. Guy shook that thought from his head and went back outside.

The heat sucked all the life from him that the diner had given back. Guy started his car, and felt the air conditioning cycle up to start pushing the cooler air. He put the car in gear, and swung around to one of the old pumps. Guy shut off the engine and got out. He looked at the pump to see if it was a self-serve, but the pump handle was some sort of weird contraption, and Guy couldn't tell. He tried to read the faded words on the pump, but it was the same strange lettering that had been on the bathroom sign. It didn't even have any numbers Guy could understand.

Guy looked at the porch of the building, at the man standing there. He was huge, over six-foot-six, and fat, and must have weighed over four hundred pounds. He had on bib overalls over a dirty Tee-shirt, and an even filthier ball cap, with some unrecognizable logo on it. Guy saw he was barefoot, his feet hairy and lumpy, the toenails stained a dark brown. The man smiled, exposing a horrendous mouthful of teeth, yellowed like aged ivory, some missing, the black gaps repugnant. A well-gnawed toothpick tilted from the corner of his mouth.

"So you want some fuel to git where you're goin'? I'll pump it for you. I'm used to the heat." The man's voice was a gravelly rasp, scraping upon the hearing like sandpaper.

"Yeah, thanks. Fill it, please."

"I'll check the oil and belts, too. Why don't you check out the Killer Snake Farm and the curio shop?" The man pointed with the toothpick. Guy shrugged and walked around the building.

The curio shop was simply a shack, and inside were wobbly tables covered in junk. Odds and ends of all kinds were stacked haphazardly, with old tools, piles of yellowed newspapers and magazines, bottles, jars of colored fluids with floating lumps. Guy did not want to know what was inside them. There were a few stuffed animals, and several more skeletons of others. Some of the skeleton animals had extra limbs and odd shapes. One table held an assortment of framed photographs. Guy took a casual look at a few, seeing sepia-toned old pictures that could have been taken in the Wild West, and one, in fact, showed a hanged man.

Guy started to turn away, but his eye caught a black leather frame, with a date on the photo of 1896. The photo showed twin girls in white dresses. Each wore a ribbon in her hair, but of course the color of each could not be determined. Guy held it, seeing the likeness, and felt a shiver of fear trickle down his spine. He set down the picture.

In the corner was a small, unmoving, white-haired figure in a rocking chair, wrapped in a Navajo blanket. Guy couldn't tell if it was a dummy or a real person, and didn't want to get close enough to find out. He closed the door of the shack behind him as he walked out into the dazzling sunlight.

"Seen the killer snakes yet?" The big man was standing close, wiping his hands on an oily rag. Guy was so close that he could smell a peculiar, vaguely unpleasant odor coming from the man. He wanted to move away.

"Uh, no."

"Come on, then."

"I, uh, really have to--"

The man stopped, and looked directly at Guy. "You tellin' me you got to be someplace else? That you caint take a minute to see my Killer Snake Farm? It bein' free and all?"

"No, not at all. It's just brutally hot out here, and--"

"Won't take but a minute," the man said, taking Guy's arm and leading him the rest of the way. Guy could have pulled free, but the man was easily twice his size, and Guy did not want to offend him. They stopped in front of a dozen large glass cases, under an overhang of rusty sheet metal.

Guy obligingly went from case to case, but all the snakes were flatly coiled and motionless, or completely hidden. He looked at the hand-lettered card identifying each snake. The type of snake was written in English, and underneath, the oddly lettered symbols.

"Say," Guy said to the man. "What is that writing? What language is that?"

"Don't rightly know," the man shrugged. "This place is real old. It was here when we took it over."

"Maybe it's Native American?" Guy ventured. "Navajo or something?"

The man ignored him and looked down at a small animal which had come up alongside. It put its paws up on the man's leg, and he reached an arm down to scratch it behind the ears. Guy thought it was kind of like a dog, but there was something strange about the creature that he couldn't put his finger on.

"What kind of dog is that?"

"Mixed breed," the man muttered. The animal loped off, in a half-sideways movement that made it seem like it had had a leg broken and not quite healed.

Guy spoke. "You said 'we'. I take it you're Jerome, and the man in the diner would be Mr. K?"

"He's my brother."

Guy was shocked that the two were related, being so absolutely different. He swallowed. "How long have you had the place?"

17

"A long, long time," Jerome said, seeming to look off in the distance. "What do ya think of the snakes?"

"Well, not really much to see, is there? They seem to all be sleeping, or comatose."

"You want 'em riled up and spittin', that it? Movin' around, all dangerous, like? Cause they ain't snakes unless they's movin' around, ready to bite? They're plenty dangerous, even when they look like they're sleepin'. Wanna stick your hand in and find out?"

"No, but--"

"What about if I feed one? That satisfy ya?"

"You really don't have to--"

Jerome pulled something white from the pocket of his overalls and held it up. Guy saw it was a live mouse, and the man held it by the tail, dangling it. The paws spread, the desperate creature trying to grab onto something solid. Before Guy could stop him, Jerome opened the top of one of the cases and dropped the mouse in. It stayed frozen in the corner of the case, whiskers quivering, nose twitching. Jerome grinned at Guy and rapped on the glass.

Guy saw movement of the brown coil, and then a head reared up. Black-button eyes focused on the frightened mouse in the corner, a forked tongue tested the air. There was more movement, and the body of the snake moved closer to its prey. The head lashed out, and Guy saw a miniature explosion of sorts as the fangs of the snake sank into the body of the mouse. The snake settled back, and the mouse convulsed with rapid and violent twitches, until it lay still. The snake moved in, opened its jaws wide, and engulfed the head of the mouse.

Guy could not watch any more. He stepped away from the cases with a sick feeling, Jerome following.

"That's something' huh? The end of one creature's life being sustenance for another."

Guy looked at the man, surprised that he would use such a word. As if reading his thoughts, Jerome grinned back at him.

"Didn't think I knew a word like that, didja? Thought I was some dumb old gas-pumping moron."

"Hey, I didn't--"

"It's alright. Others have thought that way, too. At first." Jerome winked, and Guy felt even more uneasy. He followed the man into the office of the gas station. There was no fan or air-conditioning, and the unmoving heat was like being smothered with a heavy blanket.

On the back wall of the place was a large rack with numerous guns: revolvers, automatics, shotguns, rifles. Boxes of bullets were piles in heaps, with strays scattered about. Guy looked at them arrayed, and wondered why someone would need so many.

"Want one?" Jerome was grinning at him.

"What? A gun? What for?"

"Odd jobs."

"Like what?"

"Ending things that have gone on too long."

Guy was wondering if Jerome was serious, or still playing with him. The man was quiet, studying him.

"No, I don't want or need a gun."

"You sure? Do it up right."

"Do what? Oh, forget it. How much do I owe you?"

"Hunnert bucks."

"What?"

"One hundred dollars." Jerome rolled the toothpick in his mouth to the other side.

"Is this some kind of joke?"

Jerome stopped smiling. "I don't joke when people owe me somethin'."

"My car doesn't take a hundred dollars' worth of gas."

"Cost of gas is more expensive out here."

"That's still way too much."

"Feel free to go somewhere else and get it cheaper."

"So that's the game, is it?"

"Replaced your fan belt, too." The man held up a frayed black string of rubber. "It was about to go. Full tank, parts, labor. All adds up."

"Adds up to a ripoff."

The man looked at Guy. "You'da been in bad shape if I hadn't checked and replaced that belt. You'da got down the road a piece, and your car woulda died. You mighta, too. Not much traffic out there in the desert."

Guy cocked his head. "So the hundred dollars includes the fee for saving my life?"

The man smiled. "Nope. That's for free. But you can believe it, if it makes you sleep better at night. If it was, though, be a pretty damn good bargain, I'd say. And you got a nice lunch, too, which you didn't pay for."

Guy stared at him. "How do you know that?"

"I know a lotta things."

"He told me the lunch was free."

"Nothin's free in this world, sonny-jim, and many others besides. Somewhere down the road, ya got to pay for everthin'.

"Well, a hundred dollars is too much. What if I refuse to pay?"

"That would be a very bad day for you. But, I suppose I could siphon out the gas outta your tank, and give you back this." Jerome jiggled the black strip of rubber.

"This is robbery."

Jerome shrugged again.

Guy was fuming, but did not see a way out. He couldn't just run out without paying, Jerome would probably shoot him. "I could report you, you know."

Jerome smiled and put his hand to the toothpick. "But you won't."

"What makes you so sure?"

"You just wanna keep on runnin' to wherever it is you're runnin' to. Until you reach the end and haveta make a real choice. You don't wanna include me in your thoughts, except with a spit and a shudder."

Guy blinked and rocked back on his heels. "What kind of place is this?"

"Just a Roadside Attraction. A little stopover on your way to someplace different. You ain't stayin', you gotta go on until you find it."

"What? What will I find?"

"That everything you lived through can't be just dropped and forgotten. You can't run from it, you gotta carry it with you."

"This is Hell."

"Nope, just a quick stopover. Hell is tryin' to pretend things didn't happen, or killin' yourself because they did happen."

"I have nothing. Nothing but pain."

Jerome reached behind and brought out a huge revolver. He pointed it at Guy, and thumbed the hammer back with a loud click. "Want to end it, then? Want me to pull this trigger and splatter your brains all over that wall? That get you off the hook?"

"You're crazy!"

"Answer the question. Four pounds of pressure ends your pain. And everything you ever were, and all you could have been after this."

Guy looked down the barrel of the gun, and he saw a dark tunnel that stretched to forever. He made a sound in his throat.

"What's that?" Jerome's eyes were rimmed with red.

Guy was afraid. "I said no."

"No, what?"

"No, I don't want you to kill me."

"Then give me my damn money. One hunnert dollars."

Guy swallowed, and reached for his wallet. Hands shaking, he opened it up and tried to pull out some twenties. He managed to count out five of them and held them out.

"Put 'em on the counter."

Guy did.

Jerome eased the hammer down on the gun and set it under the counter. He smiled. "Will there be anything else? Or have you got enough out of your little stopover?"

"I sure have a lot of questions, and not many answers."

"People make up their own answers."

"At least tell me why you do all this."

"I don't do nuthin'. People do it to themselves, and wind up here. We offer what people need. So what else do you need?"

Guy thought about it. "I need to get out of here."

"Well, we're always open. You can always come back, make a different choice."

"No, I won't be back this way ever again."

"We'll see. You be real careful drivin' now. Can't ever tell when you might fall asleep and crash."

Guy stumbled back to his car and started the engine. He didn't think the car would take him where he needed to go. But, for the first time since the terrible thing happened, he'd have to start thinking about a real destination for himself.

Dale T. Phillips

THE GREAT SNIPE HUNT

I tale you now a story of back in the useful, youthful days of Summershine, which we enjoyed maxaloutely as we played. Being in school was cruel, but we had just been released, and were soaking up Sollyrays to the fullest. We rambled and scrambled over hillendale, and teased the toff-prof in Effigy, a spot not far away.

We had our usual group, and whensome; to wit; myself, the chronicler extraordinaire; Harold the Herald, also known as Vox Clamantis; AngelEyes ('She with the orbs of different hue, one is gold and the other is blue'); Rabbit, by nature the timid one among us; PeachPi, a mathematical genius; Athos, the strong and shylent one; and WillardWisp, our imaginary playmate. WillardWisp was by far the most popular among us, since we could lay blame for all bad luck and all depathing of goodness upon his broad but invisible shoulders. Everyone should have such a friend.

We frolicked to such games as 'Drakes and Ducks', where we took turns doing fowl imitations while the others guessed which ones we twittered, or 'Kings-and-Queens-of-Far-Off-Worlds' (my favorite, since you chose any sort of custom for the others to follow), and

'Kick the CanCan', where some of us would dance madly while the rest spoke French and pretended to drink strong spirits (all except for WillardWisp, of course, who always objected). We teased him that he didn't take his liquid in the right spirit, and he told us he was consumed with envy.

But the Summershine eventually bored through us until we were thoroughly bored. One day the fun came to a crashing not as Solly scorched us from his lofty perch. We lay on our backs, looking up at the skyhigh, clutching handsful of unsodden sod so as not to fly away prematurely. Not even a WillardWisp of a cloud with which to play Shapes ghosted the endless blue. We lay mirthless and heavyheartmore.

"We need excitement," said AngelEyes.

"A search," responded PeachPi tangentially.

"A quest!" Athos posed heroically.

"Something more," whispered WillardWisp. We waited with breath bated.

"Agreedy indeedy. We need a Hunt!" Harold heralded.

Rabbit spoke up from where he was lying down. "But what shall we hunt?" He asked, for we were not hurtful, and the thought of intentious stalking was abhorrent to us.

"Fear not, my lapinous friend," Harold went onward. "We are not hare to pursue bunny business. No, no. Our game is much more clever and elusive. We shall, this very eventide, venture forth in pursuit of the wild and woolly snipe!"

"I don't even know what a snipe looks like," AngelEyes spoke her viewpoint.

"Nor I," said Rabbit, in what, for him, was a bold statement.

"But some say they're only a legend," Athos objectified.

Those of us who weren't in the no-know had hooked our three gullible friends, and Harold warmed to the task.

"The snipe is elusive," Harold said. "And seldom seen by anyone, much less caught. Cross a ferret with a lemur with a wombat, ruffle the fur backcrosswise, and there you are, with luminous eyes, sensitive ears, and an even more sensitive nose. Their being very senseable, they are hard to catch, because they don't care for bigfolk like us, my fuddybuddies. They run with the elves, gnomes, and fairies, but shy away from such as we."

"Then how do we see them?" asked AngelEyes.

"By the JunieMoon reflection off their great shiny eyes."

"Sounds easy as falling off a logarithm," said PeachPi.

"How do we catch hold of them?" said Athos.

"Not in a trap of steel?" quivered Rabbit.

"No, no, of course not," soothed Harold. "Extraordinary creatures cannot be caught by ordinary means. Else you'd see pet snipes everywhichwhere: in stores, on leashes, in cages, in fine restaurants. Which would be a most horrible thing, as they are very sensitive and delicate.

"You must wait for the Eve of Believe, which, however, comes this very night," Harold continued. "You use specialsoft snipe sacks, carefully rubbed with civet and fennel in the moonlight, to discombobulate the keen proboscis of the snipe. Lastly, to get the snipe to enter your sack, you must say a special charm over it. It has to be a personal charm, one no one else hears or knows. It must be very powerful, full of belief. If you don't believe, the snipes will dash right by you, over, about, and through you. But with a strong belief, a good charm, and a stout soft sack, you just might be lucky enough to coax one in. Once in the bag, we shall marvel at the wonder before releasing the snipe back to the JunieMoonlight games."

"How do we go about it?" asked Athos.

"We'll divide up," said PeachPi. When we groaned at her, she smiled sweetly and told us she was nonplussed.

"Since Rabbit, AngelEyes, and Athos have not yet caught a snipe, they shall be the baggers," said Harold. "The rest of us shall be the beaters. We shall flush the snipes and send them bagwards, as you stand there holding the mouth of your sack open and waiting. Our whistles shall alert you that the snipes are coming. You'll close your eyes, repeat your charm, and Presto!"

"Won't it be dark and scary, though?" asked Rabbit.

"You'll have Lunalight aplenty sitting on your shoulder. With Athos and AngelEyes as co-vigilmates, you'll have nothing to fear."

"To the hunt," whispered WillardWisp.

"To the hunt!" We bayed like hounds until Harold bade us cease.

"This calls for a celebration race."

"Yes!" We roared, leaping up to sprint for the clubhouse.

"Last one there is a witches' lunch!" We whooped as we swooped away.

It was a marvelous race, the heat of Solly ignored. When speed gave a lead, another would overtake them. Fast as cheetahs we made it to the clearing and tore across the dotted line together.

"Dead heat!" We howled in glee as Solly agreed.

"And just as it should be. The witches shall dine on none here this day," Harold gasped. "To the swimming withall."

We leapt up again and dashed to the pond, to roll like otters in the waters. Later we emerged to collapse in the Sweetgrass, laughing as Solly dried us. We wrung our clothes and hands until Athos heroically scrambled up the ladder to the clubhouse, and returned with a blanketed bundle.

With solemn ceremony, he spread the blanket on the ground, revealing a dark, musty bottle and a set of tiny teacups.

"Alice in Funderland," we cried with glee.

"I'll be the Cheshire Cat," purred WillardWisp.

"I can see me as Alice," piped AngelEyes.

"It adds up that I should be the Queen," said PeachPi.

"It's the Mad Hatter for me," said I, with a trace of madness.

"Who better than me for the Mock Turtle?" mocked Harold.

"Caterpillar," said Athos, waving antennae.

"But," we looked around in mock panic. "We have no White Rabbit! We simply cannot play without one! Who can we get to play the White Rabbit?"

"Well, er, how about me?" Rabbit stammered.

"You!" We thundered, feigning surprise. "Why what a brilliant idea! A Rabbit you are, and a Rabbit you shall be! But hurry up, you're late."

"Oh dear, oh dear," Rabbit murmured and looked at his watch. We dissolved into helpless laughter, as we did every time we played. Then we arranged ourselves and poured the DoughnutWine, the bottled liquid essence of Baking Day. We waited as Harold held up a hand and raised his cup.

"A toast," he said. "To the Great Snipe Hunt."

We echoed his sentiment, and drank. We savored each drop and sat back contentedly. When he had finished, Harold smacked his lips and stood.

"And now we must each repair to our lair till Eventide. Meet back here when JunieMoon shows her lovely visage. I'll bring the necessary equipment. Adieu for now."

Ah, what a grand illusion and ghostly trick we were to play on our three unsuspecters. During our bushwhacking, we would call out like ferocious wildee beasts to scarify them. Their fear and feet would be fleeting, and merry we would be. Explanations and we would follow about how snipes as such were imaginery only.

We regathered when Lunalight lumined the clubhouse. Harold solemnly passed a snipesack to Athos, AngelEyes, and Rabbit.

"Here is your sack," he intoned. "Guard it well. Has each of you a charm?"

Nodding heads bobbed, and Harold went on.

"Once set in position, you must stay like a statue, for any movement will spook the poor snipes. No matter what your ear might hear, you must not move, or all will be lost." Harold winked at us. "And don't believe those silly stories about wolves eating snipehunters."

"Wolves?" Rabbit quavered.

"Yes, wolves," Harold went on, matter-of-factly. "Large ferocious carnivorians with dark fur, hypnotizing yellow eyes, and huge, sharp teeth that devour small, furry creatures, and sometimes humans. They have a rather long, lamenting howl, especially when they're on the hunt. But fear not, for no one's parts have been devoured by a wolf in these parts for quite a stretch."

"What about that boy they didn't find?" asked PeachPi, dangling the angle.

"No evidence he was wolfed down," Harold replied haughtily. "And even if he was, the one who did it probably isn't even around here anymore."

Our baggers and baguette displayed concerned expressions of impressions. The seed of doubt had been firmly planted, and later we would try to bloom it to full flower.

Whippowhirls twittered distantly, and flyerflies buzzed around us in the nightish air. We led our glum chums to a small clearing in the goodwoods where their faces were clearing in the Lunalight.

"Here in this space is your waiting place," Harold said. "Now open your ears, allay your fears, close your eyes, and be armed with your charm. Make ye ready and remain steady. Remember, you must truly, truly believe. Forget fear, forget all else. And most importantly, don't even think of wolves at all."

Poor Rabbit groaned.

"Now, Rabbit," Harold said. "That feeling will keep you snipeless. Now off we go, to drive them fro."

"Keep your eyes peeled for theirs," I cited.

"Keep your sacks low and spirits high," added PeachPi.

We crashed through the goodwoods until we could laugh without being heard. Once chuckled out, we slipped silently back to spy, as invisible as WillardWisp. Our friends cast nervous glances surroundingly but not surrenderingly, and bravely stood their ground like summer knights.

31

PeachPi made a ghostly hoot.

"Wh-wh-what was that?" whispered Rabbit.

"Owl," offered Athos, swallowing hard.

"Don't they eat rabbits?"

This mirthed us mightily. I hollowed my hands and rolled out a deep, rumbling cough.

"Now what was that?" asked a very quivering Rabbit.

"Maybe a bear," said AngelEyes.

"Oh-h-h," was all Rabbit could say. We made light of their plight, and saved the worst for last. Harold tilted back and gave out with his best howl, rending the night and icewatering the blood. White with fright, our stalwart companions still held their ground and their sacks.

We stick-whicked the thickets, and mauled shrubbery as we shouted.

"There's one! Watch him, Harold!"

"PeachPi, behind you! There!"

"They're coming your way," we called. "Must be a whole nest of snipes here!"

And so on until we entered the clearing, prepared to display our disappointment at their snipe-catching failure. But our friends squealed with glee, and danced for Joy, who was not there.

"We've caught some!" they shouted.

"What?" We answered, blunderstruck at the error.

"Snipes. We've caught snipes!"

We disbelieved them. Were they trying to best our jest?

"But snipes don't really exist," said Harold. "There are no such things. A snipe hunt is a hoax to hex the baggers."

"Then what are these?"

Three sacks each held a small, furred creature with luminous eyes, large alert ears, and a very nervous expression. We looked at each other, then back in the sacks.

"This is impossible," sputtered Harold.

"You said if we believed, we would catch one," Rabbit spoke up, to the brim with confidence. "With the right charm, you said, they'd run right and left into our sacks. And that's just what they did. Oh, we were terribly frightened, but we believed."

We were dazed and amazed, shocked out of talk. And then the topper arrived in the shape of a huge wolf. He strolled into the clearing with red tongue-a-hanging, yellow eyes-a-blazing, and white sharp fangs-a-clicking.

Three sacks fell at once. The snipes hurry-scurried in a rash dash to the bushes. Chasingly, the wolf followed, while we ran full tiltingly in the other direction. Once safe behind tall walls, Harold gaspingly turned to Rabbit.

"You really believed there was a wolf out there, didn't you?"

"Well, of course," answered Rabbit. "But there was."

"There wasn't until you conjured him up by believing, just like the snipes."

And thereby ends a tale, but not our adventures. However, we nevermore went out hunting for snipes. And evermore from that point on, we were very, very careful of what we believed in.

Dale T. Phillips

THE TREE OF SORROWS

Mallory stood alone in the night, watching the thick fog swirl around him like a shroud. He had made the long, cold walk onto the Golden Gate Bridge from downtown, and he was tired and numb, which suited him fine. Somewhere down far below was water, but what he truly sought was oblivion. He had debated on whether to be or not to be, and decided Hamlet had chickened out. At this point, he felt like he couldn't do much worse.

Cars sped by on the bridge, the noise coming to him as if wrapped in cotton. The chill of the dense wet air cut into him, but it didn't matter. He expected to taste a greater chill shortly. Mallory savored the feeling, looking down once more to where the water should be. How far down? How long would he fall? How did that old joke go? The fall won't hurt, it's that sudden stop at the end.

He fished in his pocket for a cigarette, resisting the comparison to a condemned man. He looked at the cigarette for a moment, remembering that they were called coffin nails. Mallory thought it was the height of irony that this cigarette was lengthening his life instead of shortening it. At least he wouldn't die of lung cancer.

He shouldn't have thought of death, for Karen's face came back to him, plain and clear. The memory cut him with razored edges, and he tried to push it back before it all came spilling out. He lit the cigarette and drew on it savagely, taking in too much smoke. He coughed harshly for a minute.

Mallory spat the cigarette out and crushed it under his foot as if it were the cause of all his troubles. He wondered what had ever made him take up the filthy habit in the first place. Sometime back in school, probably. He thought it was odd how casually people picked up things that figure so prominently in life without ever realizing the effect they will have.

Ah, might as well get it over with, he thought. He reached out and gripped the bridge railing. It was cold and wet to the touch, and as he pulled his hands back in surprise, he noticed it was also very dirty. So what? Didn't matter either. He stepped up to try again.

Footsteps were coming his way through the fog. Mallory cursed the fact that he couldn't even do this right. He panicked and stepped back from the rail, not wishing an audience. He turned to face whoever it was. Plenty of time after they left.

Be funny if it was a mugger, though, huh? The guy could pull a gun or knife and Mallory would laugh, telling them to go ahead, he was going to jump anyway. A real riot.

A small figure came into focus out of the fog. It was a man, and he walked to within a few feet and looked at Mallory. "Please don't do it," he said.

"What?" Mallory was astonished.

"Jump. You were going to. Please don't."

"What the hell are you talking about?" Mallory said.

"I realize you are in pain and going through a difficult time, but this is not the answer," the little man said.

"Who in the hell are you?" Mallory asked.

"No one special," the man said. "Just someone who would like to see you rejoin humanity."

"Humanity and not society, huh?" said Mallory bitterly. "At least you're not a social worker."

"Oh, but I am, in a manner of speaking."

"Great," spat Mallory. "Well, you've done your good deed for the day, so why don't you run along?"

"I don't think that would be a very good idea," the man said. "You're still contemplating taking your own life."

"How do you know what I'm thinking?"

"It's written all over you, my young friend," said the man.

"Don't call me that," Mallory said flatly. "I don't even know you. You are, however, starting to piss me off."

"I'm sorry," the man said quietly. "But you see, you don't have to die now."

"I don't know what your game is, fruitcake, but you better beat it before I loosen some of your teeth."

"I don't think you would do that," the man said. "Your anger is directed inward. But if you do, I will do nothing to defend myself. I could not and would not stop you. But you don't seem to be a cruel man."

The little man was right, and Mallory felt foolish. Tears stung his eyes. "Look, what is it you want from me?"

"I want you to rejoin humanity."

"You said that before," Mallory said. "What do you get out of this?"

"The satisfaction of seeing you live again."

"My living is over," Mallory said woodenly. "It ended in a hospital room one month ago."

"Ah," said the man. "Your wife?"

"Yes, since you're so bloody interested."

"And you want to rejoin her," the man stated.

"No," Mallory replied quickly. "I don't believe in any of that stuff."

"Then why must you take your life?"

Mallory looked at the man, astonished. Why was he talking to this jerk, anyway? He tried to give an answer that wouldn't sound foolish or sophomoric, but couldn't. He said nothing.

"Because you think there is nothing left worth living for, right?" said the man.

"Yeah," said Mallory. "You got it."

"Let me ask you something," the man said. "How long did you know her?"

"Six years," Mallory admitted. "Look, I really don't want to talk about this."

"But you were alive and living before you met her," the man insisted.

"Listen, damn you!" Mallory burst out. "Karen was the best thing that ever happened to me. I watched for eight months while she died, a little bit each day. And I died right along with her. So don't you tell me life is beautiful and all that crap, because I don't buy it. You can't bring her back. Now I'm tired, I'm cold, and I'm in a lot of pain. So save your breath and whatever crusade you're on for someone else."

The man was quiet for a minute, watching Mallory intently. "What if you could trade your pain for someone else's?"

"What?"

"Would you trade the pain you feel for someone else's pain?"

"You are one crazy old coot," Mallory said, shaking his head.

"To forget your bitterness, forget that familiar ache, and take on someone else's in place of yours," the little man said.

"Man, no ones' pain is worse than mine."

"So you would, then?" the man seemed almost eager.

"Yeah, if it will make you happy, yes, I would."

The man seemed happy at the pronouncement. "Then come with me, and we will trade that pain of yours for that of another."

"I don't believe this," said Mallory. "You are nuts, plain and simple."

"But you have nothing to lose by coming with me."

"Oh, hold on a minute," Mallory shook his head. "You probably think you're the devil, and you want to trade my soul for this deal, right?"

The little man laughed heartily. "Oh, no, my young friend, nothing of the sort. The only devils that exist are the ones inside each person. Your soul is your own, don't worry. The only deal I offer you is to trade your sorrow with that of another, but you can always have your own sorrow back, whenever you wish."

"You're not kidding, are you?" asked Mallory. "You really do believe all this stuff."

"As I said, you have nothing to lose by coming with me."

Mallory sighed. "Well, I guess you're right there. What the hell. Lead on, old man."

"Excellent. Please follow me."

"This just beats all," said Mallory.

The man started walking toward the Marin side of the bridge. Mallory shrugged and followed.

They walked for some time through the clinging fog, and Mallory was tired. He was just about ready to call off this whole screwy deal when the man stopped beside a parked car and told him to get in. It was just an ordinary car, nothing special, and Mallory checked to make sure there was no one in the back seat.

They settled in the car, and the man drove carefully through the fog dancing around the vehicle. Soft soothing music came from the radio. Mallory got comfortable in the bucket seat. The ride was smooth, he was tired and worn, and with nothing to see out the windows, he was soon asleep.

Mallory woke when the man turned the engine off. He rubbed his eyes and oriented himself, seeing the man and remembering. The fog still enveloped them.

"Shall we go?" the man asked him.

"Where to? Where are we?"

"We're at The Tree of Sorrows," the man replied solemnly.

"Where?"

"The place where you will rid yourself of your pain, and take that of another."

"Oh, right," cracked Mallory. "Well, let's get to it then."

They got out of the car, and the man led Mallory through the fog, which began to thin out, except for a thick ground cover. Mallory wondered how far they had driven, thinking it might have been several hours. His fatigue was gone, and this place didn't look like anywhere near the Bay. Maybe they were somewhere in Yosemite.

As the fog thinned, Mallory looked up into a red sky. It was not just the horizon, but the whole sky overhead was lit like a darkroom. Mallory was puzzled, and wondered vaguely if the man had slipped him some sort of drug.

They were on a broad, flat plain of some sort. It was barren except for one outstanding feature which Mallory saw up ahead. It was an enormous sprawling tree, with branches close to the ground and reaching up to a height of twenty feet. The branches spread out for hundreds of feet, coming off the main trunk, which was twisted and gnarled.

Mallory had never seen anything like it, and was impressed as well as a little afraid. Everything was deathly still, and the tree seemed to be sentient somehow. Mallory looked at the little man, who gazed up at the tree with an expression of reverent awe.

"This is the Tree of Sorrows," said the man in hushed tones. "Come here."

Mallory stepped forward. He could reach the branches with his outstretched hand. He saw darkish lumps like strange fruit hanging heavily from the branches.

"Reach out your hand," said the man, and Mallory did so.

"Move around with your hand out," the man told him, almost whispering. Mallory began to walk, slowly, as if he were feeling his way in the dark. One of the lumps glowed as he passed his hand near it.

"That's it," cried the man. "That's the one."

41

The man reached past Mallory and pulled something from the branch. He held it out, and Mallory took it. It was a rough, solid ovoid, slightly larger than a melon, and heavy, with a wrinkled skin.

Mallory thought it resembled a giant raisin and smiled. With a start he realized how long it had been since he had found anything truly amusing.

The man looked at him with a searching gaze. "Yes, that is it," he spoke. "The sum total of all your worldly sorrows, throughout your life. All your trouble and pain are contained within. That's why it is so heavy. Squeeze it and see what I mean."

Mallory put pressure on the sides, and a little puff of air came through a hole in the top. The loss of Karen came flooding back, and he felt the hurt. But there was more, as every disappointment, every lost chance and lost loved one came to mind and tore at him. Mallory almost dropped it in his grief.

"Seems like a lot, doesn't it?" said the man. "Walk around and try another. When you come to one you want, pull it down and replace it with yours. That person's sorrow and troubles will then be yours, and you will have theirs."

Mallory wasted no time and chose one close by. Pulling it down, it seemed smaller and lighter than his. He squeezed it to see what it was like. With the escaping air came a cascading of memories, of the thoughts and dreams of another. There was pain, confusion, and despair.

Mallory recoiled in shock, and hastily replaced it. He looked over at the man, whose expression was unreadable.

Perhaps it was too close to his own. He stepped several feet away and tried another. Again came the puff, and the tumbling thoughts. This one had a wide, solid feeling of bitter hopelessness within. It was duller than Mallory's, without the sharp edges, but was more wearying. Mallory shook his head and replaced it, again looking at the little man who revealed nothing.

This time Mallory walked a good distance and reached up high to bring one of the strange things down. He was overwhelmed by loneliness, a terrible, aching yearning that made him feel pity for someone besides himself for the first time since Karen's death. This person had never known love in their entire life. At least Mallory had had some good years with Karen. He put the thing back with care, wondering how that person kept going.

Mallory kept trying, with a dogged determination. He was shown such misery as he never thought existed. He lived through the worst of failure, betrayal, disease, hate, and disaster. He saw the suffering of childbirth without the joy, and saw shattered lives from all types of tragedy.

The smaller ones he had thought would not be as bad, but they felt too uncomfortable. He could not accept them as his own. Each time he replaced one, he understood a little more about the human condition.

Mallory finally stopped, realizing that further search was futile. There was no sorrow he could choose to replace his own. The pain was still there, but it was sharp because life had been so good before. Some of the ones he had tried had so little good throughout. He walked back to the man.

"Well? Did you find one?"

"You know I didn't," Mallory said quietly.

"Why not?" asked the man.

"Because there was nothing that was mine. My troubles belong to me, and I think I can deal with my pain now. It still hurts like hell, but I can grieve and live. But what about them?" he gestured at the laden branches.

"Everyone suffers," said the man. "The way to alleviate that is to find joy. You're not the only one to feel a loss like the one you've had. You can help others now, for every bit of happiness can make these lighter. There are many who add to this Tree, but there are many more who do their best to make things better for others. Every person who realizes this and cares can change things. You are one of those people now. I'll take you back, and you can rejoin the living."

Mallory followed the man, but turned to take one last glance at this terrible, yet very human place, bidding a silent goodbye. He went back to life, knowing that he had, in a way, traded his sorrow. And he thought it was a very good bargain indeed.

THE CATS OF ATHENS

Nothing was as Jim Bloom had imagined it. Ever since he had arrived on the shores of Greece, he knew he was in a different world altogether. Throughout the rest of Europe he had used his phrasebook to get by, with fragments of language and a few basic words. But now he was an illiterate child, staring at a sign like the village idiot, unable to decipher the simplest words.

A triangle was a delta, he knew that, but other than that it meant nothing to him. Everything looked like a list of fraternities and sororities. He was forced to rely on English translations and charades. He was in the land that had spawned his civilization, and he was unable to comprehend anything of it.

Pictures still translated, though. The open and pervasive pornography shocked him, even after the relaxed standards of European nudity. In the gift shops and on the street wares, there was an overwhelming display of naked protruding appendages, stamped on postcards, vases, booklets, everything with a remotely flat surface.

The city of Athens, that pinnacle of the Periclean Age, was another crowded, noisy, dirty, modern city. There were traces of stone ruins and marble statuary in places, but the acidic air pollution was rapidly eating away what past remained.

And the wine. This culture had worshiped it, if not created it. They had a God of Wine, Dionysus. So why did their version taste like a version of boiled horse urine? Both of the two types of wine, retsina and demestica, were completely unpalatable to Jim, who was able to quaff most beverages of an alcoholic nature. Even the hard liquor of Greece was awful, for ouzo had licorice as its base, something Jim could not abide.

And their army was head-scratchingly contradictory. Their soldiers looked fierce, and they carried sub-machine guns, but they wore little skirts with pom-poms and tassels. Jim wanted to laugh. How could you not? The uniforms looked like silly schoolgirl outfits.

But one thing Jim did love was the bazaar. This was where the old Greece began. The place was a huge collection of small shops, crammed together in an unorganized jumble. Jim walked the winding lanes, watching the haggling between the shopkeepers and the buyers.

A group of boys had a cat trapped in an alley, and were preparing to kill it in some entertaining way. Jim shooed them off, ignoring the incomprehensible insults. The cat looked at him as if acknowledging a bond, then escaped down a side path.

Jim climbed the nearby hill to the Acropolis, exploring every crevice and cranny, feeling centuries of history soak into his being. He took a swig of water and watched a group of tourists look around, seemingly without any comprehension. They stared open-mouthed at their guide, and gazed blankly at columns and stones. They moved like cattle, lumbering slowly from one spot to the next. Jim thought that to them, the sacred hilltop might as well have been a ruined shopping mall.

Jim tried to imagine what the ancient Athenians were like. A people that invented democracy, and yet kept slaves. He wondered how the mind compartmentalized like that. But still, Periclean Greece was one of the few places where the word of a poor man was equal to that of a rich man. Jim rued the series of civil wars of the Peloponnese, which bled Greece dry and led to its ruin.

The afternoon sun was oppressive, and Jim sought refuge in a lonely shaded corner. He found a recess in one of the stones where he could not be seen, and laid down next to the cool stone. His weariness overtook him, and he slept.

Hours later, Jim awoke with a start. His eyes were open, but he couldn't see, and he realized it was dark. He came from his place of refuge to a world awash in moonlight. There was no sound, and the stillness was eerie. The monument had become a city of the dead.

Jim's feet crunched on the dry soil, and he felt like a ghost moving through the ruins. Then he heard a sound and froze. When guards carried sub-machine guns, it was smart to be very careful when you were illegally in a place after hours. He shuddered at the thought of being caught and having to deal with the local justice system.

The closer he came to the sound, the more he recognized it as chanting. Now he could see a half-dozen naked people, arms outstretched to the moon. He sucked in his breath, astonished and embarrassed.

As he watched, transfixed, a cat approached the group. It changed in to a man and joined the chanting figures. Jim wondered if he was still dreaming. He couldn't possibly have seen what he just thought he saw. Perhaps it was a trick of the moonlight.

Two more cats came close, and they suddenly became a man and a woman. Now Jim was sure he was hallucinating. He took a step backward and froze. Sitting there atop a broken pillar at about waist height was the cat he had saved earlier in the day. The cat watched him with luminescent eyes, and Jim wondered if the cat had followed him, or had appeared by chance.

He felt he must say something, but his mind was not up to the task. He got out a strangled "Hello," and his voice sounded odd. The cat turned into a woman, and Jim was totally speechless. She was beautiful, her eyes held the same cat-like luminescence, and he no idea where to place his gaze, as she was completely naked. The woman stepped lightly down from the pedestal, graceful and lithe, and spoke to him. At least he thought she had spoken, but her lips had not moved.

"You are uncomfortable," he heard in his head.

"I've never met a goddess before," he thought back. Remembering what had happened in mythology to the young man who had spied the naked Artemis, he was afraid.

"Do not worry," she said. This time she spoke aloud. "We will not harm you."

A man detached himself from the group and approached them. He looked at Jim and then at the woman. Jim's head carried the exchange.

"Shall I disremember him?" he stretched out a hand to Jim's head.

"No," the woman spoke again. "He is the human who saved me."

The man nodded and bowed, and moved off to join the others.

The woman smiled at Jim and spoke this time, her lips moving and the sound coming to Jim's ears rather than inside his mind.

"Thank you for saving me today." Her voice was like a soft Vivaldi concerto, sending a thrill through Jim.

"You're welcome," he responded, having found some of his composure and voice. "But couldn't you have easily got away?"

"We accept certain inconveniences. One is a physical form. No, you truly saved me from harm. So I would not allow Bel'aika to touch your mind. Though we do not allow humans to see us thus."

"I can understand why."

So looked at him and chuckled softly. "You are uncomfortable because I have no clothes. Every one of you comes into the world without clothes, yet you find shame in not wearing them."

Instantly she was clothed in a gauzy shift, which seemed to flow in the moonlight. A word came to Jim's remembrance: gossamer.

"Who are you?" His voice was pure wonder and marvel.

"We are the ---," she had said a word which Jim could not pronounce or understand.

"Where do you come from?"

She pointed up in the sky behind him.

"We have lived among you for many of your centuries. We had hoped you would grow as children age and learn, and someday join us. And so we took these forms and lived among you."

"All cats are your folk?"

"Not all that you call cat are of us. But all of us have taken that form."

A thought flashed through Jim's mind.

"Is that why people think cats have nine lives?"

"Yes."

He nodded. "So why are you here at the Acropolis?"

"We are going home."

"Home? Back to—" Jim pointed back the way she had, at the stars.

"Yes."

"So we've grown up?"

She looked at him solemnly. "No. Your planet is dying."

"What? How?"

"Neglect and destruction. You destroy everything, including each other. You foul your food, your water, the very air which keeps you alive. Even the whales suicide themselves on your beaches to protest. What more evidence do you need?"

"Can't you help us?"

"We have been trying for thousands of years. We first came to the land you call Egypt."

"You came as cats. And you were revered as gods."

"Yes, we showed them many things. What did they do with the knowledge? They created vast empires, with war after war. They spent their energies and resources to create huge tombs for their leaders. And those leaders squabbled amongst themselves. They fell prey to their nature. Then some others came to that land, soldiers from here."

"Alexander's army," said Jim. "They started a line of pharaohs."

"They had the rudiments of civilization. So we followed them back here, to see if we could encourage them to improve. They developed democracy, but excluded their women, and kept slaves. In the end, they seemed more interested in slaughtering each other, and so they faded from the world scene.

"And then came the Romans. But everything we taught them was applied to weaponry and war, and they used their knowledge to conquer others. They had law and learning, but they grew arrogant, and believed they were invincible.

"After them, we were discouraged, and it took centuries to build useful knowledge. We were able to spark a rebirth."

"The Renaissance," Jim said.

"Yes, so much happened in such a short time, you even have a name for it. The human spirit made great gains, and the benefits went on for hundreds of years. But again, when any group did well, they invaded their neighbors.

"But we kept hoping and working, and again there was a rapid blossoming of learning."

"The Enlightenment," Jim said.

"See? You recognize how wonderful and useful is the knowledge you've gained, but you instantly begin to misuse it. Everything we taught you turned to more efficient ways of killing your fellow beings. We do not understand this lust for slaughtering each other. We fail to see how you think you gain by such a thing. Whenever a great being comes among you and gains fame by telling others that it is better not to fight and kill, you destroy them."

To his regret, Jim was able to come up with a number of examples without having to think much. Jesus, Gandhi, Martin Luther King, Jr.

"And so we are leaving."

"You're giving up on us?"

"More than half the people on your planet live in poverty and misery. But they continue to reproduce, bringing in more people to suffer. So we are leaving you to yourselves. We regret that what we have taught you was used to injure others. Perhaps if we had left you with rocks and clubs it would have been better, as you might have stopped short of exterminating each other.

"In spite of everything we are fond of you, and you have great promise, if you could keep from committing planetary suicide. If you continue down the path you seem bent on, the results will be more horrible than anything you can imagine. We cannot take any more. How can you watch a beloved child deliberately walk over the edge of a cliff?"

"You could make us stop war."

"If war is your ultimate desire, that is your destiny, and your destruction. If killing others and killing yourselves is all you have learned from your thousands of years of existence, and that drive is more powerful than all others, then it is your fate. You are children who continue to put your hand in the fire, long after you have learned that it burns and produces no benefit.

"You do not remember any lessons from one generation to the next, even after you developed writing. You all march toward the cliff, always thinking one step closer cannot hurt, until you tumble over the edge."

"Couldn't you take over?"

"Yes, we could rule you, but that is not our way. You are ignorant and savage, but you feel, and some of you are capable of great things. And so we must take our leave."

Jim was quiet. "Are you going to do something to my mind? Make me forget?"

"To what purpose? If you were to speak of us to others, they would call you mad or a liar. There are many others who have visited your world, and yet those who speak of them are outcast. Even some of your leaders, and people whose very lives depend upon their responsible reporting, have told you time and again of visitations. As a species you do not believe them, but yet you believe in fantasy beings for which there is no proof. There is an odd madness within your species."

"I could tell people. I could write it as a story, a parable. Maybe they would listen."

The woman smiled at Jim, kindly, but sad. "What did your kind do to the very best one among you who spoke of a better way and talked in parables?"

Jim hung his head.

"But your action today was a start," she said. "Saving a lower creature from harm is a sign of great compassion and holds promise for your future. Goodbye James Bloom. Perhaps you will change the souls of your kind to inspire them to be what they can be. We hope so, we truly do."

She gently stroked his face, and turned to go. The shapes shimmered, glowed, and slowly faded away.

Jim stood alone in the moonlight, amid the ruin of a fallen world, his tears dropping into the parched, ancient soil. He wept for all that was lost, and wondered if there was anything he could do to bring his world out of the darkness.

Dale T. Phillips

THE WATCH OF THE YELLOW EYES

When Talbot first saw the house on the bluff overlooking the ocean, he was struck with the thought that his dead wife Lynnie would have loved it. It had a Gothic flavor, all stonework and sea backdrop and lonely seclusion. Massive pillars of rock guarded the road that lead up to the house, with a stout chain and a 'No Trespassing' sign. The driveway was a long, tree-lined path that thinned out to the barer place atop the cliff.

The total isolation of the place had drawn Talbot. He didn't want anyone around, not the sight or sound of other people. Here was only the pounding of the surf below the cliffs, the wind howling against the windows. Here in this wild, rough place he might find the peace he sought.

Talbot's only companion was Marvel, a beautiful Irish setter with a lustrous coat and bloodlines of canine royalty. Marvel was listed with the American Kennel Club and had even won a few shows, but Talbot no longer did that. They were companions in sorrow now, not teammates competing for prizes. Marvel received the only affection Talbot was able to muster now for anything.

Talbot didn't know anyone from the quiet Maine village, and he came in late September, after all the tourists had left. Here Marvel would have room to run, here Talbot wouldn't have to talk to anybody. The few locals were taciturn and would keep away. As a measure of his wish for privacy, Talbot replaced the chain at the outer gate after he had driven through. He didn't want anyone to come by unless he called them for something specific.

There was still an hour of daylight left when he pulled up to the house for the first time. He let Marvel out, who then scampered joyfully all over, thoroughly berserk with glee at all the new smells. Talbot smiled to watch him, the first smile in a long time. He used the key in the front door and went indoors to find the lights.

The inside was plain and simple, practical New England standards of no-nonsense, no frills furniture. There were places where you could sit yourself down comfortably, but it was not set for style. The fireplace was built of small stones painstakingly cemented in place. There was some kindling and a few chunks of firewood set in the carry basket next to the fireplace.

The kitchen was small, but Talbot didn't mind, as he had only himself and Marvel to forage for. Upstairs, he knew from descriptions, was one bedroom and another room Talbot could turn into a work studio. He looked in the smaller space and satisfied himself that it would make a serviceable workroom. But the bedroom had a four-poster bed, perversely like the one he and Lynnie had. She would have loved it, even to the down comforter on it. The memory made Talbot suck in his breath. He bowed his head, but there was nothing to do for it. He would have to sleep here, no matter what memories it conjured up.

Talbot went downstairs and unloaded the few groceries he had bought on the way through town, and put them into the refrigerator. Tomorrow he would go to the big supermarket, many miles away, and stock up on everything. Tomorrow he would unload all the car, not just his overnight bag and a duffel bag of clothes. He was careful to bring in the shotgun, though. Wouldn't do to leave that out in the car. He set it in a corner, and dumped the handful of shells into a drawer.

Talbot cooked supper for Marvel and himself. He opened one can of chili and one of dog food. There didn't seem any great difference between the two. He set out Marvel's dish while his supper was heating. Marvel happily dove in, tail wagging, noisily chomping. Talbot ate his chili silently. Since Lynnie died, food was another thing he had lost interest in.

After supper, he turned on the outside light and opened the door for Marvel to run for his nightly doings. Marvel was in the yard, sniffing all the new exciting smells, when suddenly he stopped. He gazed at a point in the woods, and his hackles rose as he emitted a low growl.

"What is it, boy?"

Marvel barked once, and looked back at Talbot.

"Go ahead, boy. Go get him."

Marvel raced off into the darkness, barking furiously now. Talbot heard him crashing through the underbrush, claiming his territory by chasing off the intruder. Marvel came trotting back minutes later, tail wagging in victory. Talbot grabbed him by the ears and rubbed him roughly.

"Good boy. You scared him off, didn't you? Yes, you did. Good dog."

Talbot let him explore a few more minutes and mark the area until the cold started to get to him. They went back in, and Talbot built a fire in the fireplace. The little blaze was cheery, and helped dispel the gloom. Talbot read until he got sleepy, and went up the stairs after he closed the grate of the fireplace and turned off the downstairs lights. He looked at the bed with sadness, but slept in it anyway. His dreams were naturally of Lynnie.

The next day dawned bright and clear. Talbot unloaded the car, and spent the morning getting things put away. Around lunchtime, he decided to go for the groceries, and loaded Marvel in the car. He drove for close to an hour, to the town closer to the highway, one that had enough people in it to warrant a supermarket. Talbot spent a long time getting everything he thought he might need. Marvel sniffed at the bags when Talbot put them in the car, but Talbot had bought a bone chew-toy for Marvel, who gripped it and worried it, ignoring the groceries.

Talbot drove back to the house. He tried to think of the new place as home, but it wouldn't come yet. He tried not to remember that he was running away and hiding. There was the big project he could fool himself into justifying. After all, one needed peace and quiet for research and contemplation of a project this size. That was the real reason, Talbot said to himself. Nothing to do with getting away to a place where no one would talk to him, remind him.

Talbot was out with Marvel walking near the cliffside at sunset. Talbot suddenly wondered why he shouldn't just run out over the edge. The rocks below could end his pain and loneliness. It would certainly be termed an accident. It was an easy way out. Talbot gazed out over the edge, listening to the pounding surf, wondering if he could do it. The more he thought about it, the better an idea it seemed. An old rock 'n roll song came to him, "Endless Sleep", about how the sea called people to drown themselves in it's waters.

Marvel barked furiously at something in the trees. Talbot was startled to his senses, and shook his head. He looked at Marvel, who was rigid, convinced his mighty bark alone could roust the intruder. Talbot urged him on.

"Go get him, boy."

Marvel raced off into the trees. Talbot realized that if he did hurl himself into the ocean, there would be no one to take care of the dog. That wouldn't be fair to Marvel, who had been a good companion. So the decision was put off for now.

Marvel came back, eager for approval, and Talbot lavished it. He ran his fingers through the dog's coat.

"You're a lifesaver, sport."

It was a few days later, with the rain coming down hard, that Talbot once more thought about The Question. He was doing nothing, interacting with nobody, so there seemed little reason left to go on. He couldn't even cry. His numbness was complete. He sat looking out the window until it got dark. Marvel came in and nuzzled him, looking up expectantly. Talbot realized he had to feed him. It got him up and moving. Once he had fed the dog, he thought about feeding himself. He knew he should eat, but he had no appetite. He stood with his hands on the sink, unable to move, unable to act.

Now Marvel whined at the door. He wanted to go out, despite the hammering rain. Talbot let him out, and stood motionless on the porch, listening to the rain. It was a lonely sound, and once again Talbot began thinking of ending his loneliness. There was the shotgun, after all, sleek, black, and deadly.

Marvel had found something else to bark at, and didn't stop. Talbot came out of his reverie and peered through the curtain of rain, into the darkness.

And he caught sight of a pair of yellow eyes staring back at hm from the dark.

Fear paralyzed Talbot, a mortal, primeval dread. It was the first time he'd felt fear since Lynnie's diagnosis. He tried to call for Marvel, but could make no sound. The eyes disappeared. From out in the darkness, there was a yelp of pain. Unfrozen, Talbot turned on the light. It's comforting gleam shone out through the silver downpour, as Talbot kept calling for his dog.

Finally, from out of the treeline, Marvel came limping. Talbot ran to him, oblivious to the soaking. Marvel had a bloody paw, and Talbot knelt beside him, speaking soothing words. He picked Marvel up and staggered back to the house.

Inside, he took a towel from the closet and thoroughly rubbed Marvel until the dog was dry. Talbot inspected the paw, which had stopped bleeding. He changed into dry clothes and built a roaring fire, thinking back to primitive man holding back the terrors of the night in the same way. Talbot got the shotgun from the corner, and took his time carefully cleaning and loading it.

That night, for the first time, Talbot let Marvel sleep on the big four-poster bed with him, the shotgun nearby. He wondered about the eyes, and what sort of creature it was that he had seen. It had to be large, and it had injured a large, aggressive dog. Could it be a wolf? There couldn't be any of those left in this part of the country. Inland, possibly, but on the ocean's edge? Maybe another dog, then. Yes, of course, that was the simple answer. Talbot tried to calm himself with this rationale, but his sleep was troubled.

The next day, Talbot took Marvel to a veterinarian, whose number he had found in the outdated telephone book. The vet inspected Marvel's paw, put some disinfectant on it, and said it shouldn't be a problem. When he got home, Talbot called the town animal control officer, who was not in. Talbot left a message on the machine, telling how his dog had been attacked by something large, with yellow eyes.

When he got back, Talbot checked the grounds for any traces of other animals, but found none. He had been hoping to come up with some proof of what he had seen. Discouraged, he went back inside and made lunch for Marvel and himself.

As Talbot was cleaning the lunch dishes, a truck pulled up outside. Talbot realized he had left the chain down at the roadside, so someone had driven in. Talbot took Marvel and went out to see who it was.

"Mornin'." A cheery little man in a green jumpsuit greeted Talbot as he got out of the truck.

"Can I help you?" Talbot said.

"Might be t'other way around," the man chuckled. "Animal control. Bob Jenkins. You called me."

"Ah, so I did."

"You left a message about seeing somethin' big? Hurt your dog?"

"That's right. This is Marvel. I took him to the vet, and he's okay. No way to tell what attacked him. I took a look around, but didn't see anything."

"Most likely some other dog. I ain't seen or heard of anybody's getting loose, but I'll keep an eye out. Mind if I have a look around?"

Talbot did mind, but thought he'd better cooperate.

"Of course. Go right ahead."

Jenkins spent about twenty minutes tracing over the same ground Talbot had, and with the same result. He came back up to the house, slapping gloves against his pant leg.

"Can't really see anything, not surprising after all that rain. You call me if you see it again."

"I will, thank you."

"Alright. Good day now."

When the man left, Talbot walked down to the gate and rehung the chain. It was like pulling up the drawbridge on a castle.

For a number of days, Talbot sat in his converted office among the clutter of his papers and books, trying to muster some enthusiasm for his Big Project. He was attempting a study of Aeschylus, but without his heart in it, he could do nothing. He sat hour upon hour looking at the stacks of notes with colored tabs indicating pages of former interest. Now they were as dead leaves. He wanted to put his head in his hands and simply weep without stopping. The Question kept looming in his head.

One night was exceptionally quiet. Talbot had built a fire and fed Marvel, who lay curled and contented. Talbot sat in the big armchair and looked over at the shotgun in the corner. When he at last turned back, a pair of yellow eyes stared at him through the window. He jumped, alarmed, and Marvel jumped up with him, barking at the sudden movement. The eyes were gone, and he could see nothing in the windblown gloom outside. But he had seen them, that he knew. Something was out there, watching him. A long coil of fear snaked down Talbot's back, making hm shudder.

The next morning, Talbot called Jenkins again, and the man promised to come out. When he arrived, Talbot told him of the huge yellow eyes staring right through the window, bold as brass. Jenkins seemed skeptical, but took a look around. He came back, looking displeased, and cocked his head at Talbot.

"You sure you didn't just see a reflection? Maybe headlights in the window?"

"I saw them," Talbot said with heat. "There's no headlights you can see from those windows, they face the sea."

"You weren't by chance having a nip or two?"

"I don't drink." Talbot's voice was ice. "I take it you don't believe me."

Jenkins shrugged. "I'm sure you saw something. It's just that we get outta-staters up here, they're out by themselves a little while, they go a bit stir-crazy, start imagining things, or making things bigger than they are. Had a hunter once, thought he'd shot a bear, brought it in to the ranger station, wanted it tagged. It was a black Labrador retriever."

"I'm not an idiot."

"Good. Then explain to me how there are no tracks, no scat, no sign of prey carcasses, as would be from such a large predatory animal. There's no cover on this point for anything big."

"Well, don't wolves range in territory? Maybe it came from elsewhere."

"Wolves?" The man laughed. "You gotta be kidding me. We ain't playing Little Red Riding Hood here."

Talbot flushed.

"Well, something big is out there." Talbot snapped. "I don't want it attacking my dog again."

"Alright, don't get sore." Jenkins rubbed his chin. "I can set a coupla traps." Seeing Talbot's look, he went on. "Humane ones, I mean. Big suckers, I got some out in the barn. Little rusty, but they should still work."

"Thank you."

"That's my job." Jenkins walked to his truck. He opened the door and turned back. "I'll come by later, set them out."

And so it was that several hours later, four large steel wire cages were set out and baited. Jenkins showed Talbot how they worked.

"You don't want a raccoon or anything small getting to the food. So it has to be something heavier, which means bigger, to push this door open to get in. If there's something out here, it'll come for the free food. It's like a lobster trap, because once they're in, they ain't getting' out again."

That night, Talbot realized he was waiting for the traps to vindicate him, showing the animal he had seen. But there was more. In his involvement in the issue of capturing the animal, Talbot had got interested in something. In getting interested in something, Talbot had put off The Question.

The next morning, Talbot all but bounded out of bed, eager to check the traps. He and Marvel went outside, and Talbot saw that all the food used as bait

64

was gone, from all four traps, though there was nothing caught. He phoned Jenkins once again, who came out and inspected them. Jenkins narrowed his eyes when he looked back at Talbot.

"Never had anything could get the food from these and get out again. This mesh keeps out the little critters. Maybe something small could have wormed into one, but not all four."

"Then how?"

"Only way I can figure is human intervention."

"What, like someone--"

"Are you playing some kind of game with me, sir?" Jenkin's face was white with suppressed anger.

"What?"

"Are you messing with me? Because I do not take kindly to it."

"I assure you, nothing could be further from the truth."

"I cannot stand bored outta-staters who play games with us here in town because they've nothing better to do."

"Now look here," said Talbot.

"I'll bait 'em back up," said the man slowly. "Maybe you got some kids funning around, but if not, I got to be real suspicious when I see all four unescapable traps all sprung at once with nothing in 'em."

"I had nothing to do with this."

"I ain't sayin' you did," the man said, looking back toward the sea. "I'm just sayin'."

Though Talbot was outraged, he realized how energized it made him. He took Marvel in the car and drove forty miles to a hardware store, and bought motion-detector lights. He spent the rest of the day setting them up, training one on each trap. He also dug into his boxes that had lain unpacked since he'd arrived, and found his camera equipment. He selected a high-end model, loaded it with film, and set it up on a tripod, pointed at the trap, facing out to sea. He set another loaded camera close to the big chair. Marvel sat with head in paws, watching his master and the sudden flurry of activity.

By the end of his labors, Talbot discovered he was hungry. He had had no appetite for the longest time, but the effort of the day had made him ravenous. He cooked a big supper for himself and Marvel, and laid out the table with real dishes, rather than eating out of the pot like he had been doing lately. He was surprised to rediscover how good food tasted, and even indulged himself with a bottle of wine from the half-case he had left.

After he had cleaned up, Talbot seated himself to look out the picture window, where he could just see the outline of the trap. He readjusted his camera, and rechecked the shotgun to make sure it was loaded and ready. Then he settled down to wait.

But the meal and the wine and the outpouring of energy had taken its toll, and Talbot fell asleep in the chair. He awoke to barking, and jumped up to see the motion detector light shining on the trap, which was turned over on its side, despite having been staked down by Jenkins.

Talbot grabbed the camera and the shotgun and banged out through the door to the porch. As he did, the motion detector light shut off, and Talbot could not see in the sudden dark.

As he stood there waiting for his eyes to adjust, Talbot felt a presence. It was not menacing, it was somehow... comforting. It wasn't Marvel, he was inside. No, it was something odd, but a little familiar in part, mixed with other things: sadness, pain, longing.

Time seemed to slow, the very air felt thick and unworldly. The light went on again, and there it stood: a full grown wolf, a female, Talbot guessed. It looked neither hurried nor surprised to be so pinned by the light. It stood facing Talbot. There was a sound from behind, and Talbot looked back to see Marvel upright, with his front paws against the picture window, watching with rapt attention. But Marvel was not barking, as he should have been. Talbot turned back to the wolf, who had not moved. If Talbot had thought this creature to be malevolent or harmful, he sensed none of that now, only the vague pains he had been surprised to find come forth. It was almost as if... but no. That could not be.

Talbot looked into the eyes of the wolf, and all his memories tumbled out. Everything up to Lynnie's end. Then Talbot added the rest, coming to this place. But there was a cloud in the line, the thing that was not to be spoken of, or named correctly. It was simply The Question. Talbot squirmed a little as the wolf seemed to gaze at him with pity and sadness.

He was alive, Talbot realized, and seeing the wolf in this form before him helped him know he must not do what he had come to this place to do. He must go on, with all the painful memories carried within him like a war wound that would not heal, to the natural end of his days. No shortcuts allowed.

Talbot set down the camera and walked out to the wolf, holding the shotgun loosely, pointed away. He reached out and touched the dark fur, feeling the roughness. He kept walking, out to near the edge of the cliff. With the shotgun in both hands, he spun it out over the cliff, to where it would shatter on the rocks below, and The Question with it.

Talbot looked back, but the wolf was gone. But it would always be with him, had saved him. He straightened his shoulders and went back inside the house. Tomorrow he would rejoin the world.

YESTERDAY AND TODAY

Corman awoke with a clear head and no confusion, all ghosts of the past in their proper places. It was heady and frightening to be this lucid again. Corman lay on the bed, carefully sorting memories, pleased when none dragged him down another tributary of the past. He lay in an unfamiliar room that had no reminders, no traps to lead him into the shifting maze of times before. The room had an odd, musty smell, but not one that triggered any memories.

Corman was therefore not surprised to find himself alone in the bed. Unlike so many other mornings, he didn't expect any wives or lovers he had once known. Naked, he sat up and swung his feet to the floor. The cool surface felt good. Corman stood and stretched, his 200 years feeling light on his healthy, muscular body. His bladder alerted him with pressure, and he went to relieve himself. The disposal unit wasn't working, but he used the imitation porcelain out of habit.

Returning to the bedside, he looked around the room. There were no loose items, other than his clothing and knapsack. He checked the Autostore unit by habit; it was of course not functioning. Corman rummaged in his pack and came up with a container of food. The preservatives left his mouth dusty and dry, but there was no liquid to wash it down with. His trip to the relieving room had been disappointing; water had not flowed through to these rooms for years.

Corman tried to open the window. The mechanism was unfamiliar and fairly ancient, but with determination he created an opening. The sky was an ugly, pallid gray. Corman couldn't remember the last time he had seen a blue sky. There were so many things he couldn't remember. He could see the street, but detected no movement. He judged himself five stories up, and wondered what had possessed him the previous evening to climb five flights. Corman pulled on his jumpsuit, shouldered the knapsack, and left the room.

Despite the leaden sky, Corman felt good. In the open air, he pondered what to do. He had no idea how long he had before the random access of PreSen deposited him in some hole of times gone by. Finding he recognized this part of the city, he began walking toward the park.

There were no people about, which disturbed Corman. Despite PreSen, this had been a populous city; somebody should be visible. He noted the dismal decay, the weeds poking up through the streets. The wind blew cold, vengefully biting Corman through the jumpsuit's insulation. It was late Autumn; Winter was not far away. More people died in Winter. Some were suicides, others just wandered out into the cold. These bodies, seemingly forever young, could still be halted by neglect.

Corman looked around, and realized with a start that he was near to where he had met Linda. He wondered if she was still in the old place. It was dangerous, thinking like this. She had been so important in his life that seeing her or the old place might flood his precariously balanced mind with overwhelming memories. He probed his own thoughts delicately. The blessed sense of the present was still with him. He shrugged, and decided to check if she was still around.

The old place, the place he and Linda had shared for so many years, was in a once-fashionable area. Even this district suffered from the decay infecting the rest of the city.

Several blocks from the old place, he saw a husky man standing in the street. The man looked down one street, then slowly turned to look in the opposite direction, his expression that of a child. Corman knew he was lost, in both time and place, and walked over to him.

"Hello," he said.

The man peered back at Corman, looking puzzled. "Where am I?"

"South side of the city, by the causeway. Do you know where you live?"

The man thought a moment. His hands, thick and strong-looking, fluttered aimlessly. The movement looked out of place on him. He seemed about to cry.

"I... I don't know." He jammed his hands into his pockets, seeming to be ashamed at forgetting.

"It's okay," said Corman softly. "The only was I remember is with my Card." Corman pulled the metal rectangle from his own pocket and held it up for the man to see.

"You don't happen to have yours on you, do you?"

The man frowned at the piece of metal in Corman's hand. He searched his pockets, scowling. His face lit up as he brought forth the shiny Card and proffered it to Corman. Corman took the Card and read it.

"George Martin," he announced. "Hi George. My name's Corman." He stuck out his hand.

"How ya doin'?" George pumped Corman's hand and grinned, eager and friendly, like a big dog.

"Good, George, good. Your Card says you live not too far from here. I happen to be going that way." The lie came easily. "Why don't I walk with you?"

"That'd be great." The big man looked vastly relieved. He took his Card back and followed Corman, chatting happily. He spoke of owning a car, back before they were banned. He made it sound like a very short time ago, but Corman hadn't seen a car in over seventy years. He couldn't recall the last time he had been in one. He didn't try too hard, for fear of slipping back. He was glad the man still had his Card on him; a stroke of luck these days, really. The Cards had been issued when Premature Senility, or PreSen, was finally acknowledged as a legitimate illness.

Corman remembered getting his Card, which emitted a beep if he got more than two meters away from it. In spite of this, some people still lost theirs. At first, the Caretakers would patiently find the person and return the Card, but eventually they lost control of their own memories, and drifted away like the rest. Even the Card could not remind people strongly enough about the present.

George talked about his family, who lived with him in the suburbs. He told how they had to take care of his mother, apparently an early victim of PreSen. A cloud passed over the man's features as the mention of PreSen shuffled his memory.

"That was a long time ago," he said apologetically. "Sorry, I forget sometimes."

"We all do now, George," Corman said.

George turned quiet. Corman knew he was trying to get back into the present, treading carefully, like Theseus through a maze.

They rounded a corner onto a broad boulevard, passing empty skeletons of skyscrapers. With everything so quiet, the sky could have been a comforting blanket, but Corman saw it as a shroud. Depressed, he looked out over the collapsed causeway, and saw several birds flying over the water. The sight gladdened him.

They turned twice more. Corman checked the numbers to find the correct one on an old brownstone. He stopped. George stumbled, looking up at the broken windows and the crumbling steps. He turned and peered at Corman suspiciously.

"Who are you?" he asked.

"Just someone passing by," Corman replied sadly. "You live here, don't you?"

The man flinched as if struck. He looked up again at the faded building.

"Yeah, I guess I do." He started up the steps, pausing before going in.

"Hey!" he called. Corman had started to leave, but turned back at the man's call.

"You helped me, didn't you?" George said.

"Just walked with you, that's all."

"No, you helped me. Thank you for that." The man's frame sagged as he opened the door and went inside. Corman shivered and walked away.

He walked back to Linda's neighborhood. The streets remained chill and quiet, with no one about.

Corman navigated the emptiness, wondering where all the people had gone. Surely things hadn't got this bad?

On a corner, Corman recognized a restaurant where he and Linda used to go. He looked at it for a moment, the memory of it washing over him, but not taking him away. He shrugged and looked for a way in. There was little chance of actually finding food in the abandoned building, but he wanted to check it out.

The windows and front of the building were covered over. Corman saw no way to pry anything loose. He went down the narrow alley alongside the place. Several feet over his head, a window looked promising. Corman searched for something to stand on. He found a door off its hinges and dragged it over. It was missing several central panels, but had a sound frame and looked sturdy enough. Corman propped it up with the base against the other wall of the alley. He put his foot on the frame and boosted himself up. The door sagged threateningly, but held. Using the frame in the middle, he was just high enough to get at the window.

Corman spent several minutes cleaning the filth from the sill so he could get at the window. It opened inward when Corman pushed against it, then something snapped and it swung wide. He swung his legs up and hung suspended on the ledge, peering inside.

Part of the ceiling had given way. Muted gray daylight seeped into the place, allowing Corman to see. It was an easy drop to the floor, with no obstacles. Corman hung onto the ledge, easing the lower part of his body down the inside wall. He stretched full length and let go, landing without problem.

His eyes adjusted to the gloom. This had been the kitchen. A good place to start, he thought. Methodically he searched for food. Although the place was bare, someone might have left something behind. Corman opened doors, checked under shelves and equipment, and found the big walk-in coolers. Of course they no longer worked, and none yielded so much as a scrap of food.

Corman walked through a swinging door to an empty dining room. He tried to remember what it had been like with tables, chairs, and decorations. He shook himself, recalling how dangerous such reminisces were. The sound of dripping water filled him with hope. He hunted for the source.

The water came from the collapsed portion of the roof, which left a large hole over the former bar area. The heavy wood partition still stood, but the bottles and paraphernalia were long gone. Corman saw the water fall, heard the splash. He looked behind the bar. One of the sinks was full. Corman ran to it, hardly believing his luck.

The sink had been clogged with filth, but that had settled to the bottom. The roof must have only recently given way, or there would have been more damage. The sink overflowed with inviting rainwater bounty. Corman cupped his hands and scooped some to his mouth. It was brackish and metallic-tasting, but seemed drinkable. Corman bent and greedily slurped from the surface. When he had his fill, he remembered a container in his knapsack. He took it out and filled it. There was plenty of water left, but full of debris that had been stirred up. He decided to enjoy the rest and quickly got out of his jumpsuit. He washed his face, and was able to get most of his body wet as well. The water felt good on his skin. Still wet, he pulled his jumpsuit on and continued his search.

Corman found no food or useful supplies. The place had been stripped clean. He took a last look, remembering when it had once been a busy, entertaining place. Now it was just another monument. Corman went back to the kitchen and pulled a steel worktable to the window. He scrambled up and out, and used the door on the other side to step back down into the alley. The air was fresher outside, and Corman took a deep breath, savoring it.

What were the chances of finding Linda at home in the old place? You never knew. People kept returning to places they hadn't lived in for years. Since he wasn't far away, he would at least try.

He made his way through rubble and weeds to the apartment building. Once housing the rich and privileged, it had gone to seed in a shocking way. The front door was smashed. Corman pushed his way in. Refuse choked the hallway, and he had to climb over decayed garbage to reach the stairs. His apartment had been nine flights up, but at the top he wasn't even winded.

Corman tried to remember the last time he had seen Linda. It was spring, and he had brought her flowers. That had been his last good, clear-minded day. He couldn't recall, exactly, but knew that it had been years. Corman shook his head in disbelief. When a person was lost in the vast libraries of the mind, with two centuries to draw on, it was hard to find a way out.

Passing one door, Corman noticed a horrible stench. The door was open, so he went inside. In a chair by the window sat a woman. Her decayed body was the source of the smell. There were no signs of violence. She must have just sat down and waited for death to take her. Corman recalled finding many like her, and shed no tears. Instead, he made a thorough search of the place. He found three ancient packets of food, two of which were still good. An incredible find. Corman almost whistled, until he remembered the body. When he left, he cleared the trash from the jamb and closed the door tightly.

Corman came to the old, remembered door. He had lost his keys long ago. He thought he heard a noise within, and tried the doorplate. It was unlocked. He pushed and entered. Linda sat in a chair by the window, staring out. The resemblance to the dead woman's position sent a shiver down his back. Linda turned and rose. He saw a moment of confusion before the past kicked in. She swooped upon him and they hugged.

She looked good. She had the face, body, and voice of a young woman, but was over a hundred and fifty years old. In times gone by, Corman would have been a mature man long before she was born. That changed when society succeeded in extending the lifespan by any and all means.

"How are you?" Corman asked.

"Fine. How was your trip?"

"Trip?" Corman's hopes sank.

"Of course. Washington, wasn't it?"

Corman thought back. It had been an important business conference, back when they were married, before people started going into PreSen. They had been together almost forty years. More than most. He decided not to confuse her.

"Not much to tell, really. I'm just glad to be back. You look great."

"Shall we eat out to celebrate your return?"

Corman thought of the deserted, wind-blown streets. She was in a good mood, and he didn't want to spoil it.

"Why don't we eat here? Just the two of us."

"All right. I'll fix something. Would you like a drink?"

"Sure," Corman responded automatically, before he realized she didn't have any liquor. He almost dared hope; his mouth ached for a highball glass with ice clinking merrily. As she checked the cabinet, he went to her.

"Never mind, I'm not really thirsty." He hugged her again.

"That's odd. I bought a bottle of scotch just the other day. It's not here."

Holding her tightly, Corman almost cried. 'No, my love,' he thought, 'you haven't bought scotch for decades, and the man who sold you that last bottle is probably dead.'

"What's wrong?" She said. "Honey, what's the matter?"

"Nothing. It's just so good to see you again."

He kissed her, and she responded. The embrace felt more passionate; Corman felt himself stir with desire. He thought about fighting it, and gave in. She led him to the bedroom.

Afterward, Corman lay entwined with Linda, loving the feel of her next to him. They had drifted slowly apart, like continents, when the PreSen began. One or the other would forget and be gone for long periods of time. They had stayed together as long as they could, fighting and forgetting, until they were lost. In the past, death or divorce separated couples. Now PreSen did, slowly, insidiously.

How many others, Corman wondered? People were now ships cruising on oceans of memory, each individual a Flying Dutchman, sailing aimlessly through centuries. Was anyone left who wasn't afflicted? He looked up at the window, closed and draped against the outside world. There wasn't much to see anymore.

Corman awoke, and felt Linda's absence from the bed. He sat up. She stood at the foot of the bed, in a red silk kimono he had given her years before. He knew there was a problem. Her stance was defensive, and she regarded him with a cool stare.

"So, Mr. Big Shot. Come waltzing in here and expect to pick up where you left off. I suppose you expect me to sit around here waiting until you decide you want to wander back for a quick one." She snapped out the words, hard and angry.

Although Corman knew she was remembering a long time ago, when they were breaking up, her words cut him, and he blushed furiously. She turned her back on him.

"I thin you'd better go now," she said.

"Linda." He tried.

"What? You're going to tell me you're sorry? That you forgot to come home again? How many times have I heard that one?"

"Yes, I forget!" he shouted. "We all forget now."

"That's a new one."

His words had not cut into her frame of reference. Corman almost wept with frustration at not being able to defuse her anger.

Linda rifled through her dresser.

"I can't even find my damn cigarettes!" she sounded close to tears. Corman knew the only place she could have found a cigarette was in a museum.

She turned to look at him. "Oh, are you still here?"

Resigned, Corman got up and dressed. On the kitchen table he left the two packets of food he had found. He said goodbye, but she didn't answer. Corman left the apartment, his former wife a mad bird in a cage built by her own mind.

Corman walked the empty streets without purpose. He kicked at rubble aimlessly. He tried to remember when they had hunted for a cure, when people could retain their sense of time flow for more than a few hours.

PreSen, they called it. Young bodies with old minds going senile before their time. The fragile human brain, unable to stand more than a century and a half of stored memories before shuffling them all like a deck of cards. Where were the children? He remembered that people had stopped having them. Plenty of time for that later, with all of the biological advances. But when they got older, they couldn't remember to have them.

He walked without pattern, thinking. Someone shouted to him. He looked around; no one on the street. He heard the voice again and looked up. Someone on a rooftop waved to him. He didn't look familiar, but Corman decided he might like some company.

He found the fire escape still workable, and made his way to the roof. At the top, he saw the remains of a rooftop garden, and an old man who seemed to be planting seeds. Was it possible? Corman couldn't remember the last time he had seen an old-looking person; everyone went to the rejuvenation clinics.

And seeds! Where had he found them? But the old man was wasting them by planting them now; they would die in the winter. Corman looked up at the cold gray sky, and felt an immense sadness. Maybe he could return later and dig the seeds up and save them for spring. If he remembered.

The old man was humming a tune. Watching him plant, Corman was reminded of a scene from a play, when live theater was still performed. The man worked on his knees beside an old wheelbarrow. He looked up, smiled at Corman, and rose, dusting off his knees. He walked over, pulling off the work glove from his right hand. He offered the hand to Corman, who shook it in surprise.

"Name's Arnold Matheson," the man said. "Pleased tameetcha."

"Corman. What are you planting?"

"Everything."

"Everything?"

"Yep. Beans, carrots, tomatoes, radishes, cucumbers, got some squash over there, even some corn."

"Where did you find it all?"

"Been savin' 'em. Quite some time now. My own special project."

"Why plant them now? Corman asked, careful of the reaction.

The old man looked at him. "You mean, on account of it's already Fall?"

"You mean you know Winter's coming? You're wasting them deliberately?" Corman was aghast.

"That's right."

"But why?"

"Because I'm dying." The old man walked to a crumbling edge of the roof and sat down.

"You can't be serious. Nobody dies from disease anymore."

"No, they don't. They just roll up into little balls and waste away, or jump out of high buildings. I know. I've seen 'em." The old man shook his head.

"I don't understand."

"My mind, son. My mind's going."

"Well, mine too." Corman said, after a pause. "But I'm not dying."

"What do you call it, then?" The old man's eyes were a watery blue. Corman had no reply.

"What do you call it when everything people lived for is taken away? When they go through the day playing out pieces of their life like a jumbled-up movie? When they have no more life in them but to live out the past? What in hell do you call it?"

The old man was shouting in anger, but he was crying as well. Corman could say nothing. The old man went on.

"I have nothing left. I have no future, only scattered bits of the past. I kept these seeds and myself alive for years, while everything else fell apart. Now I'm falling apart. This is the last thing I can do to make myself happy, to take a real, conscious act in the present."

He paused and looked at Corman squarely. "You take a person's mind, son, you've taken everything he was. The rest is just s shell. You've all got real pretty shells, but there's nothing inside. No reason to go on. Just keep playing those tapes until you slide into blessed darkness. We wanted to be gods; we just didn't realize the gods are mad."

Corman thought of the woman in the chair. He thought of Linda. He tried to reach back, to remember his boyhood, the golden summers, the smell of the sea. He realized the old man was shaking him.

"Do you see? There's nothing left."

The old man turned and walked away. Corman watched him go back to his knees, digging in the cold soil. Corman felt weary, and old, and afraid. He climbed back down the rusted fire escape.

The sea. He had always liked the sea; he would go there now, thinking about what the man had said. Rain pattered on him as he walked. Two streets away, a woman played in the rain like a child. The sight saddened him. Worse, however, was the knowledge that he would soon be lost again. He walked toward the sea, wondering how much time he had left.

Dale T. Phillips

NIGHT OF THE ANNOYING DEAD

When the zombie apocalypse finally came, it didn't go down like we expected. Sure, the dead rose from their graves, all rotting and nasty, and shambled around everywhere, moaning so loud they'd drive you crazy. But they weren't hungry to feast on the brains of the living. They just wanted to go back to the lives they'd lived before they died.

So all over the world, the loved ones of the departed got quite a shock when the deceased came back home and tried to rejoin the family. Hell of an inconvenience. Ever have a zombie knock down your door and try to kiss you like they were still alive and fresh? Ugh. Graveyard breath is something you really don't want a whiff of. Sure you could whack them on the head, put them out of their misery once and for all, but a lot of families couldn't bring themselves to do it. Rather, they took off, and left the zombies to remain in their last place of residence. Waves of people hit the road to look for untenanted dwellings, only to meet up with waves of zombies going back to their old jobs.

Zombies wanted to get back in their old office buildings, and so smashed all the glass and battered down the doors to do so. Once inside, they wreaked even more havoc, destroying things while trying to do former jobs, with falling-off fingers and no motor skills. They'd accidentally set fires when using the break room microwaves.

Nothing much changed at the Motor Vehicle Bureau and most government offices, as dead clerks replaced the live ones. Service even improved in a few places.

But mostly it sure was some awful mess. Zombie drivers soon made the roads impassable, with wrecks aplenty, and cars every which way. People and zombies just don't mix on the roads. It was hard to know when to cross a road, too. I remember that first week, I saw a zombie Boy Scout latch onto an older lady, trying to help her across the street. She couldn't break away, and they were moving so slowly, a car finally hit them.

Recreation was difficult because of the zombies everywhere. Let me tell you, a zombie foursome plays one very slow round of golf. And anyone who tried to swim would get manhandled by zombie former lifeguards, and probably drown first. You wouldn't even take a dead Baywatch-era Pam Anderson dragging you out of the water and doing mouth-to-mouth. Playgrounds? No way would you let your kid near the little zombie girl, especially on the seesaw.

Public gatherings soon stopped, after some gruesome incidents and grisly scenes of mass horror. Zombies got in to the Paris fashion show and started force-feeding the anorexic runway models, with hideous results. That viral video went all over the world, before the stations stopped broadcasting and the power went out.

The food supply soon became a problem. Restaurants closed that first day the zombies came back, as the service was even more terrible than usual. Zombie farmers on tractors and harvesters ran them through the crops, ruining them. In the grocery stores, zombie clerks and shoppers accidentally destroyed all the food, and all canned goods were soon snapped up by living scavengers, who defended them to the death.

Things got so bad that people protested, as if they thought the shreds of government remaining would save them. They marched with signs saying things like, "Let the Departed STAY Departed," and Make Them Stop or I'll Kill Them (Again)." But when zombie Senators and Congresspersons mixed with the live members, it was hard to tell the difference.

So many people were killed outright, and lots of others couldn't take it, and killed themselves out of despair or disgust. Which only made matters worse, because they just added to the zombie population.

Some folk started fighting back. Picking them off helped some, but you felt bad, as they didn't really mean any harm. And all the head squishing gets tiresome. But it's tough to get by. For example, you find a hotel room to sleep in, and then a zombie chambermaid breaks down the door and comes to change the sheets, while you're still in them.

One bunch of survivors set up a zombie cruise ship. Hundreds of zombie tourists were lured aboard, and they were taken out to sea and stranded. Turns out a lot of them eventually made their way to land, having fallen overboard and walked along the ocean floor.

We survivors hunker down and get by the best we can. We try not to go out much, because there are still zombie insurance salesmen, and they never let go once they get hold of you. All day and all night, you hear the slow moaning. Get more than two or three and it's pretty loud. So I guess this is the end of civilization. Unless we can figure out some way of getting the zombies to just leave us alone and start a new life. Get them to let go and move on. Man, the dead sure are annoying.

KILLER ANGEL

Detective Avery Waxman looked through the one-way mirror into the next room, seeing the woman sitting at the table. He turned to the uniformed patrolman. "She doesn't look dangerous."

The patrolman shrugged. "She said she was."

Waxman sighed. "So tell me why she's here."

"My partner and I were out in our cruiser, down past the Avenue. We saw her surrounded by three bad-looking dudes, so we pulled up. Guys all took off like their shoes were on fire. We asked her if she was okay, and she said yes. She wouldn't produce any ID, said she didn't have any. So we asked where she came from, and she pointed to the sky."

"The sky?"

"Yup." The patrolman shook his head. "So we thought we got a wacko, or maybe she'd hit her head or something. We told her it was dangerous to be out in that part of town at night, and she said she was dangerous, too."

"She say why?"

"She said she could end it all."

"Like a suicide?"

"That's what we figured. So we brought her in for observation. Couldn't leave her there, anyway."

"You did good," Waxman said. "We'll take it from here. You and your partner get back to it."

Waxman blew out his breath. He had to get his energy together before he went in. He'd seen too many crazies throughout his twenty-four years on the force. The collective psychoses and brutality of mankind was grinding him down. He rubbed his face wearily, and prepared to face another street person with a head and soul full of broken glass.

Waxman walked to the room next door, gave a gentle knock, and entered. He nodded to the policewoman who stood against the wall with folded arms. He walked around the table, to where the seated woman could see him. She was young, maybe mid-twenties, sporting short blonde hair with red highlights. She wore a dark red blouse and denim jeans. He leaned over to look at her shoes, for anything which might give him a clue. She wore a pair of plain brown ones, neither cheap nor expensive-looking.

He took a seat. "I'm Detective Avery Waxman," he smiled at her, and she smiled back. "What's your name?"

"I have many," she replied. "But you can call me Pariya."

Waxman repeated it. "Interesting name," he said. "Is that foreign?"

"You might say that," she said. Her hands were folded on the table in front of her. The skin was smooth, the nails short, with no polish. Waxman saw no ring, in fact, she wore no jewelry at all. Nor did she wear any makeup, that he could tell. She was quite attractive, with lovely green eyes and clear complexion.

"Are you comfortable?" he asked. "Would you like anything to drink?"

"That's very kind of you," she said. "But I need nothing."

Waxman could detect no trace of accent. "Where do you live?"

She smiled. "Far away."

"In the sky?"

She nodded.

"Where are you staying while you're here?"

"Staying?"

"With friends? Or do you have a hotel room? Where do you sleep?"

She looked surprised. "Oh, I have no need of sleep."

Waxman cocked his head. "That's odd. Most people do." He looked at her expectantly, and she gazed serenely back at him, offering nothing more, not seemingly embarrassed.

"Pariya, what were you doing in that part of town tonight?"

"Walking."

"That is a dangerous place to be."

"Why?"

"There are bad people there who hurt other people."

She looked at him. "You are a policeman, aren't you? Why don't you stop them?"

Waxman grimaced. "We usually come into it after someone has been hurt. Most of the time we can't prevent it. I wish we could."

"Then why let other people go there, if they can get hurt? It seems strange to me, that if you know places like that exist, you allow it."

91

"It's a free country. People get to go where they want. We have no power to stop them. No right. But we can punish those who hurt others."

"So is this punishment effective?"

Waxman looked at her. "For most. But sometimes there are people who want to hurt someone so bad, they'll do it despite the punishment."

She nodded, looking a bit sad. "I understand."

"Do you want to hurt anybody?"

"Oh, no," she said quickly.

Waxman put his elbows on the table, his hands clasped together. "But you told the officers you were dangerous."

"Yes." She sighed, looking down. "It is not my choice, but it is my duty."

"What? What's your duty?"

The woman lifted her head and looked Waxman in the eyes. "I am an Annihilatrix. I have been sent here to test you. Mankind. To see if you deserve to continue to exist, or if you must be stopped."

"Stopped how?"

"By eliminating all people."

"How would you do that?"

The woman placed her hands on her stomach. "I carry the seed of destruction. If I am killed, the seed will be released, and your world will be destroyed."

Waxman sat back. Full-bore looney, no doubt about it. Poor thing. So young, and her mind completely gone like that.

"Pariya, I'm going to call somebody who can help you. A doctor."

She frowned. "But I'm not ill. I do not need a doctor."

"It would be good for you to talk to her about these things. Would you do that for me?"

She smiled again. "Yes. You have been kind. And I see that it is not always your nature."

Waxman gave a tired smile. "You can see that, huh?"

She nodded, not smiling. Waxman wasn't spooked. Crazy people sometimes had good perception about certain things, or in other cases, just made lucky guesses. She had no real idea what he was like, what he'd seen and done. Otherwise, she'd have run screaming from the room.

"Okay, I'm going to go call her. It may some time before she comes. If you need anything in the meantime, just ask Officer Inez here. It's been nice to meet you, Pariya."

"Go in peace, Detective Avery Waxman."

Waxman whispered to the policewoman as he left. "She seems calm, but be on your guard. You never know."

Inez smirked. "I got it."

Waxman looked at her. "I'm serious, Inez. I had charge of a kid once that looked like he came straight from the choir, said yes sir, no sir, like butter wouldn't melt in his mouth. Cool as a cucumber. I looked away for a second, and he jammed a pen in my neck. Right here." Waxman pulled his collar away to show the scar.

"That why you're so cranky all the time?"

"One of the reasons." Waxman hesitated. "I just don't want to fill out all the paperwork if something happens."

The woman smiled deeply, showing dimples. "I like you, too, Detective."

Waxman blushed.

"Make your call and go on home now," she said. "I got this covered."

"Yeah, I'll do that. It's been one raggedy, long-ass day."

"Ain't they all?"

***

Waxman looked up the number on his Rolodex, and made the call.

"Doctor Harrison? Detective Waxman here. How are you doing?"

He listened, and smile into the receiver. "Yeah, I know. I'm sorry it's after hours. But we have a young woman down here, got saved by a cruiser patrol in the bad part of town. No purse, no ID, says she comes from the sky somewhere."

Waxman listened again. "Yeah, says she's on a mission. Said she was an Annihilatrix, whatever the hell that is. Don't ask me to spell it. But she says if she's killed, she's got something inside her that will destroy Mankind. I'm not kidding, she really said that."

The voice on the other end asked a question.

"No, she seemed lucid otherwise. She was calm, had an even voice. She's young, attractive, polite, dressed okay, no signs of anything amiss. But you talk to her and woo-whee. Quickly goes off the deep end. I just wanted you to come down and do a quick eval on her, figure out where she should spend the night. Don't want her going back to that part of town. Anything could happen. Can you sign her over to County Hospital tonight, after you see her? You can? Great. Listen, doc, I've been on for sixteen hours, and I have to go home and catch some shuteye. So after you see her, you make the call if she should go or not. I'm sure you will. Yeah. Thanks a lot. We'll talk tomorrow."

After he hung up the phone, Waxman looked at the instrument, shaking his head. He wanted to put a night's rest between him and this day. He headed for home.

***

Later, an angry buzz ripped Waxman from sleep. In the dark, he grabbed the phone, a habit of long practice. "Yeah."

He sat up in bed. "What do you mean she's gone?" He listened. "Alright, I'll be there in less than a half-hour. If they find her before then, call my cell."

Waxman looked at the clock 1:12. Shit. Less than two hours of sleep. He forced himself to get up and dress.

***

At the hospital, Waxman was questioning the nurse on duty. "So what happened?"

The woman looked close to tears. "I have no idea. We went through procedure, she was checked in and fine. Suicide watch, just in case. She was under constant surveillance. Then she just wasn't there."

"She must have slipped out somehow."

"There was nothing on the security cameras. It's like she just disappeared."

"I'll want to review those," Waxman said. He was trying to think, but his tired brain had difficulty sparking. Where would she have gone?

95

He thought about their earlier conversation. Was she simply wandering the streets? Would she have gone back to below the Avenue? Oh, God, no. Waxman all but ran to his car.

It was Waxman himself who found her, around three in the morning. He'd put out the APB, and then called it off when he spotted her, simply walking in the night. He stopped his car a little ahead of her and got out.

"Pariya."

"Detective Avery Waxman." She was smiling.

"Why did you leave the hospital?"

"I was not sick, and I could not fulfill my mission there."

"How did you get out?"

"I just left."

Waxman looked around. It wasn't the worst part of town, but he felt vulnerable nonetheless, out in the open like this. Of course, he felt like that most places he went these days.

"Listen, would you join me for a cup of coffee? I'm pretty tired. I've been looking for you."

"Why?"

"I was afraid that something might happen to you."

She smiled. "Because you want to keep Mankind safe?"

"Let's start with keeping you safe. Will you come talk to me?"

"You will not have the doctor put me back in the hospital, will you?"

"I thought that was the best place for you. I'm sorry."

"You do not believe in my mission. Yes, we should talk."

***

Ten minutes later, they sat across from each other in an all-night coffee-shop. Waxman stirred sugar into his cup, but Pariya was not touching hers.

"Don't like coffee?" Waxman sipped, savoring the hot liquid.

"I have no need," she replied.

Waxman ran his hand through his hair, wondering how to proceed. He figured he'd at least talk to her about her so-called mission, see if he could find the root of the problem. "What makes you think the human race should be wiped out?"

"I don't," she said.

"But why your mission, then?"

"I just do my duty. As you do. No matter what it costs you."

"You think your duty is killing people?"

The woman looked at him. "Have you not done the same?"

Waxman shuddered. How the hell did she know that? Lucky guess, that's all. He tried to find the words. "What I did kept more people from being hurt."

"And the killing goes on and on, as do the pain and suffering. Your race is violent and brutal. That is why I have been sent."

"It doesn't seem fair, to wipe everyone out for the actions of some."

"You yourself have taken the lives of innocents for the actions of others of their kind."

Waxman found he was sweating. He was remembering a hot desert wind, blowing sand, and dead bodies, torn apart by the bullets of he and his comrades. She knew. Somehow she knew. He closed his eyes. "That was war."

"War," she said, drawing out the word like an obscenity. "And what did this war accomplish, with all its killing?"

Waxman, eyes still closed, swallowed. "Not a damn thing. We spent years wandering around a shithole insane asylum, shooting and being shot at, because our leaders told us it was the right thing to do."

"And now what do you think?"

"I would never do that again."

"Yet they find plenty of others who do. Your people are still killing people they don't know, for reasons they don't know, all because someone tells them it's their duty."

"But I learned. We can learn. We can get better."

"How long has your race been fighting and killing?"

"For all time." Waxman realized he had been pulled into her world, rather than making her see the illogic of her delusion. Such was the power of people like this, he'd read. They convinced you of their craziness, rather than the other way around. Maybe he needed another tack.

"What about beauty and love? Don't we deserve to stay around because of that?"

"You have many beautiful things in your world. Love is the most beautiful of all. That is why it is so puzzling you kill and destroy so much."

"Some people don't love. And sometimes we have to kill to protect the things we love."

"You should love each other more than you love killing. Then you would see a transformed world."

Waxman took a sip from his coffee, but it had gone cold. "Suppose you get into some accident, a completely random thing, no person intentionally seeking to harm you. Would you still destroy the world?"

She smiled. "I have the power to move from harm, if I wish."

"Is that how you left the hospital?"

"Yes. But you do not believe me."

"It's a pretty neat trick. Convince me."

And Waxman stared at the empty space where the woman had been a moment ago. He looked around, but no one was paying attention to him. He put out his arm to feel in the space where she had been sitting, but all was air. Waxman gulped and felt the beginnings of real fear. He had seen so much, but never had he seen a person simply disappear before his eyes. What if she never came back?

And there she was again. Waxman stared, feeling the stirrings of something like faith. "Are you an angel?"

"If that is what helps you to believe, then yes."

A killer angel. Waxman sought for words to make a case. It suddenly seemed like an urgent thing to do. "There is so much goodness in the world. I have seen terrible things. Done terrible things. The worst things that humans can do to each other. And I've spent the last quarter-century trying to make up for that. Suffering for some sense of putting things right. Of helping others so they won't suffer."

The woman placed a hand on his. "Yet you seek death, yourself, Detective Avery Waxman."

"I..." Waxman had no response. Of course she had figured that out. "But not everyone deserves to die."

"You all do, though, deserving or not."

Waxman had no response. He sat there, despairing that he was not more eloquent, that he could not promise a better world, that mankind would ever learn.

Through the door of the coffee-shop came two men. One wore a ski mask over his face and held a shotgun. The other wore a rubber mask and was waving an automatic.

"Nobody move," the one in the ski mask yelled. "This is a robbery! Everybody on the floor!"

Waxman was cold inside. He had to let the robbers do their thing, rather than risk lives with a shootout. They would take the money and go. It wasn't worth someone's life for the few dollars they would get.

But Pariya stood up.

No, thought Waxman. "Sit down," he hissed.

The woman gave him a look of such sadness and sympathy, his heart lurched. This could be the moment when his race was exterminated. All for a few dollars in a late-night robbery. What kind of world was it, that this happened anyway?

Waxman slipped his hand inside his jacket and unsnapped the safety strap on the holster of his service revolver.

"You. Sit down, bitch," called one of the robbers. Pariya stood where she was, not moving. Waxman eased his pistol out, keeping his hand in his lap, the gun under the table.

"I said, SIT DOWN." The robber walked towards them. Waxman brought up his gun, took a quick aim honed from long practice, and fired. The robber fell backwards, and Waxman stood. The second robber whirled with his shotgun, and Waxman saw that Pariya was in the line of fire. He fired once more, and leaped to shield her body as the return blast came, tearing into him.

Waxman lay on the floor, stunned, with ringing in his ears. He felt nothing yet, the impact of the blast too massive for anything as mundane as pain. Then Pariya was on her knees, cradling his head in her arms. He looked up at her. The red streaks in her hair seemed to shimmer, as if they were threads of flame. He saw her angel eyes glow, the eyes of a destroyer of worlds. But she was still beautiful, and he loved her.

"Let them live," he whispered. "Give them a chance. Show mercy. Be better than we are."

She leaned down and kissed his forehead. "We shall leave you to yourselves, Detective Avery Waxman, to live or to destroy yourselves, if that is your will. Let us hope you can do better than this."

Waxman felt cold, and very tired, as he drifted away from life.

But happy, for the first time in many, many years.

Dale T. Phillips

GOD SAVE THE QUEEN

Encyclopedia Britannica

The largest crustaceans belong to the Decapoda, a large order (about 10,000 species) that includes the American lobster, which can reach a weight of 20 kilograms (44 pounds), and the giant Japanese spider crab, which has legs that can span up to 3.7 metres (12 feet). The lobster is especially subject to size fluctuations and migrational shifts from changing ecological factors…

Thinkweb content, February

The 2012 Doomsday Prediction is based on a claimed end date of the 5,125-year Mayan Long Count calendar, which is December 21, 2012, and incorporates warnings from climate experts and other environmental scientists that the Earth has reached a "tipping point" that could generate mass extinctions, species changes, and worldwide catastrophes…

COPENHAGEN – Mar 10th

Leading scientists warned Thursday that global warming is accelerating beyond the worst predictions and threatening to trigger "irreversible" climate shifts on the planet.

Newsweek, March
Carbon emissions creating acidic oceans not seen since dinosaurs.

Chemical changes are placing 'unprecedented' pressure on marine life, which could cause widespread migrations and mutations, warn scientists. Woods Hole Oceanographic Institute reports an alarming rise in pollution in the world's oceans. As coastal cities become awash with rising sea levels, much of their trash will simply be dumped into the waters. This may have unintended consequences for sea life ...

New York Times April 15
Increasing Global Temperatures Causing Unseasonably Heavy Rains

Scientific American, May
Climate Change Affecting Species Growth and Numbers.

Scientists report population explosions, and warn of possible consequences...

Portland Press Herald Interview, Homer Merrick, Former Lobsterman, June 6th
"Ayuh, I'm out of a job. Lobsterin' used to be a wicked hahd way to make a livin'. Now the lobstahs are crowdin' right up onta the beaches. They can live on the land for quite a spell, as long as they stay wet—so all this rain ain't helpin'. Big as anything now, and I

swear they're gettin' bigger and meaner every goldarn week. Last week, one of them took some tourist's dog right off the leash."

Science Digest, June 27th

The Thermohaline Circulation, as they call the Gulf Stream, has stopped flowing before -- with a greater than 50% likelihood of a shutdown if we do not enact strict climate policies. Even a partial failure of the Gulf Stream would have huge consequences.

A combination of the rising ocean surface temperature, and the decreasing salinity, already visibly changes the movement of sea currents that depend on differences in temperature.

Associated Press, July 14th

The UN Climate Change Panel predicted a major sea level rise, which could flood low-lying areas and force millions to flee...

New York Times, August 6

Despite continued heavy precipitation and rising sea levels, some experts insist there is nothing to fear from Global Warming. A spokesman for the Heritage Foundation claimed media bias and scoffed at the fears of repercussions from man-made activity, claiming, "The only thing warming up is the Climate of Fear."

New York Times, August 22

Coastal Cities Report Heavy Flooding, Major Evacuations

Portland Press Herald, September 7th

Old Orchard Beach— Oceangoing tourists enjoying Labor Day received a rude shock, as people reported being attacked by sea creatures while swimming. National Guard units on shore worked with the Coast Guard to close local beaches, and emergency medical teams treated dozens of people for injuries, ranging from minor to severe. Rene Bourque, of Sac-Au-Lait, Ontario, lost a leg to what he claims was "the biggest damned lobster I ever saw!" Experts scoff at Bourque's claim of a crustacean large enough to sever a human leg, saying the attacking creatures were likely a school of bluefish or even a type of shark, confused by the warmer waters and ranging out of the usual habitat. Lobsters, though, have recently become a major nuisance in this seaside town, and along with the continued heavy rains, have caused a major drop in tourism, as they replace sunbathers on Maine beaches. Local businesses have closed, causing the economy to...

Portland Press Herald, October 12th
A panel from the Sane Science Society has declared their intent to disprove the recent claims of giant lobsters off the Maine coast. They set out today in the vessel Rational Thought to patrol coastal waters and gather evidence to refute what they say is irresponsible, fear-mongering.

Portland Press Herald, October 13th
The Coast Guard reports having lost radio contact with the science vessel Rational Thought. The ship was due to check in at 9:00 EST, but failed to signal, and has been listed as missing. A spokesman ridiculed questions of the boat being attacked by giant lobsters.

Popular Science January 15th

Scientists report numerous sightings of North American lobsters (Homer Americanus) further east across the Atlantic. The lobster population has undergone explosive growth in numbers and size, and a combination of factors has pushed them to expand outward, extending their habitat range for hundreds of miles. Experts speculate on what the effects will be, as…

National Star, April 30

Expansion of Bermuda Triangle?

Experts are at a loss to explain the reports of the disappearances of numerous small craft across the Atlantic. Over 500 vessels have been reported as missing in the last few months, and concerns have been raised about possible causes. Not since the days of U-boat warfare has there been such disruption and concern in maritime safety. Theories about the causes abound, from giant lobster attacks to space aliens, an expanding space-time rift, or a larger and more deadly Bermuda Triangle, now renamed the Atlantic Triangle.

Mother Jones, May

Families of missing boaters have demanded action and petitioned the world's governments to investigate the disappearances of loved ones in the mysterious "Atlantic Triangle." Air-Sea rescue missions have failed to locate any trace of hundreds of missing boats, and some groups claim a massive government conspiracy and coverup…

The Times, London, May 22

Lobster Sightings off Cornish Coast

Fishermen in Cornwall report sightings of vast numbers of North American Lobsters, as the temperature of the Gulf Stream changes, causing massive eastward migrations. Asked about the possibility of danger from the giant crustaceans, Mayor Arthur Tintagel quipped, "Bring 'em on, I say. We've got pots of boiling water and tubs of butter!"

Arkansas Traveler, June 1

As heavy rains continue worldwide, Senator Bobby "Noah" Dingle, R-LA spoke to the press today about his "Ark Project." Citing the loss of New Orleans, Miami, Los Angeles, San Francisco, and many coastal cities to continued flooding, he detailed plans for a multi-billion dollar oceangoing vessel, roughly the size of the QE II, to contain as many samples of major animal and plant life on the planet as possible. Rep Dingle claims Biblical prophecies have dictated this move, that the End of Times is coming, and that people had better "get their house in order"…

Atlanta Journal Constitution, July 4th

Tragedy struck today as Independence Day festivities at Orlando's new oceanside resort were cut short by an attack of oversized, claw-waving lobsters. George Simpson, the Mayor of Orlando, was struck down and ingested while delivering his speech, and casualties are in the hundreds. Troops are attempting to restore order and drive the creatures back into the sea, but are hampered by the thick shell of the creatures, which renders small-arms fire ineffective.

World News August 9th

The last known survivors on the island of Manhattan were airlifted out today, as the Big Apple became the Big Empty. Empty, that is, but for the thousands of giant lobsters which have overrun the city that now has become a ghost town. Many wept openly at the loss of a once-great major world metropolis to mindless destructive creatures which some call "hideous, giant sea bugs."

The Times, London, October 22

London Attacked! Giant Crustaceans Ravage City

At 11:02 today, giant lobsters swarmed up out of the Thames and began attacking people. Riots ensued as mobs raced to get away from the monsters. The horror of the destruction cannot be described, as the devastation spread rapidly.

After the marauding beasts attacked support structures, the great Ferris wheel, the Eye of London itself came crashing down, with the loss of life in the hundreds. Other noted landmarks have suffered considerably from the powerful claws of the beasts.

Says one resident, Stephen Miller of Notting Hill, "It was like a bloody Dr. Who episode. The damn things were everywhere. I never believed in all that rot, but if there is a Doctor out there, then help us. Help us, please."

Heathrow and Gatwick airports were overrun, and all major highways were soon jammed with panicked people seeking to flee the carnage. Refugees have streamed in to the surrounding areas.

So far, attempts to stop the monsters have proven ineffective. Scientists from Oxford say technology is the key to stopping these mutant creatures, and have rigged a sonic cannon, with high hopes for success, saying the ultrasound waves will drive the monsters back to their polluted waterways.

The Royal Family has been evacuated by Royal Air Services helicopter to the Balmoral Estates in Scotland.

Kansas City Star, February 14th
Continued Attacks Force World Leaders to Debate Use of Nuclear Weapons to Combat Lobster Crisis

Salt Lake City Tribune, March 17
Nuclear Bombs Dropped in Coastal U.S. Waters to Combat Lobsters

Rocky Mountain News, March 23
Lobsters Surge Onto Shores, Swarm up Mississippi River
Millions Flee Devastation

Arizona Republic News, May 5th
Matt Savelle, survivor of the Plains Wars, described the lobster's rapid advancements. "It was like the story Invasion Force they made into that hit movie with George Clooney. The lobsters seemed to be everywhere at the same time. They destroyed telephone lines, roads, cellphone towers, dams, and power plants. People had no communication, and were killed when they went out seeking supplies. We used planes, tanks, missiles, everything we had, but there was no stopping them. Those claws could cut through armor plate, and they'd smash through walls to get at the people inside. We just kept retreating and hoped they'd eventually stop, maybe at the desert or the Rockies. Now even the deserts get so much rain it can sustain them. I suppose they'll even reach Phoenix someday soon."

Las Vegas Sun, November 11th
Lobster Scourge Approaches City
Gamblers Put Odds of Survival at 1 in 1000

The Last American News, January 1
As the New Year dawns, many wonder if it will be the last one for the Human Race. Here on the North American continent, as the world's waters have risen, the Age of Man has given sway to the Age of Lobster. These giant creatures roam the land, and Mankind here has reduced it's civilization to isolated pockets, mostly in inaccessible high mountain ranges.

Around the world, other major catastrophes have wiped out all semblance of world government, and few legitimate leaders remain. Various groups have arisen in their place, from gangster-led looter mobs to armed, fanatically-religious crusaders. One noted group, The Children of Anti-Dune, inspired by a series of Science Fiction novels, attempted to gain mastery over the lobsters and ride them, with the use of well-placed hooks and ropes. The movement was soon crushed.

The Last Prophet, June 6th
Repent! Repent, you Sinners!

Behold, for I have seen the Claw of the Lord, and He Cometh for You in Vengeance! Why Hide Ye From Death? For He is nigh, and His Spreading Tail shall crush thee, and He shall harvest you in His Pincers.

BBC Live Broadcast, December 21
"This is Roland Handshaw Smythe-Wellington, reporting for the BBC. I'm coming to you live from Balmoral, with the surviving members of the Royal

111

Family, who refuse to be evacuated from the British Isles, saying they will never abandon their people.

For some time, the battle against the invading crustaceans seemed to be going well. But while RAF and land forces bravely fought off the first few waves, the creatures continue to press onward, slaughtering all in their path. The colour of their hideous, greenish-black carapaces is... wait, here they come, and they're... oh God. Men are valiantly putting themselves between the monsters and the Royal Family, attempting to slow the onslaught with the sacrifice of their lives. It seems to do little good, as the creatures simply cut them down and force their way across the grounds.

There are rifles to spare, but few enough left to use them. I... I cannot stand by and allow this. I am an Englishman, and I too, shall join the fight, though I know it means my certain death. This is Roland Handshaw Smythe-Wellington, for the BBC, signing off.

God save the Queen... God save us all...".

RUINATION BEACH

Location-- Ruination Beach

Day-- We used to have names for days, because they were different, and different things happened during them. Now, in the After, all our days run together. We no longer make such pretty distinctions. There is only today. We do not talk about the past, never the past, never what we've lost. And we do not talk about the future, either. There is only today.

Time-- No one cares anymore. Time it was, but now that's gone. Now we only have now. Amazing that such things used to matter.

Attendees-- Me, Randolph, Kissy, Fetch, Burke, Wanda, and Smiley. All that's left. A few others were about, but we dragged them down a ways and covered them with sand. The smell, you know. Gets to you, when the wind is right. Enough sand, you don't smell them anymore. So they don't count then, do they?

Maybe they did at one time, but not anymore. Not in the After. Not since they fell and didn't get up. Bit of that going around, eh?

Agenda-- The same. Same as all the nows in the After. Eat, shit, screw, play with Fetch, find something to keep your mind from blowing apart. Like the world. No, we keep it together here.

Just a day at the beach.

Kissy starts. "I think Fetch might be getting sick."
We all look. Our one-eyed friend looks back at us. He seems okay.
Kissy won't let it go. "Watch." She picks up a stick from the pile by the fire and holds it up before Fetch. "See it, boy? Here it is." Kissy cocks her arm and throws the stick. "Go get it." Fetch watches it go, and lays down with his head on his paws.
"See?" Kissy says. "He always used to."
"Maybe he's tired." This from Wanda.
"Or maybe he just doesn't foockin' feel like it," Burke says.
"He always used to." Kissy does not let things go.
"Guess we'll have to stop callin' him Fetch." Burke almost chuckles.
"Maybe his batteries are running down," Randolph says. I can't tell if Randolph is joking or not. Hard to tell. Sometimes Randolph got hurt in the head, the whole mess scrambled him up a little. Wouldn't be surprising, that. Happened to quite a few, you know. Present company included.
"He doesn't have batteries," Kissy says. "He's real."

"Who of us is real these days?" Burke is looking out to sea. "Right, Smiley?"

Smiley says nothing. But then, he never does. He is staring out to sea as well, but with Smiley, it's like he's always looking for something. Salvation? A ship? Someone to rewind the world, to before the After? Is Smiley real? We wouldn't know. We have never heard him speak, and I guess you must speak to be real in the now.

I decide to be real. "He's not sick."

"How do you know?" Kissy asks.

"Because he can't be," I say. I get another stick from beside the pile by the fire. I reach into a mostly-empty food tin and get some of the goo on my fingers. I smear it on the stick. I go over to Fetch, who watches me with his single eye, like a Cyclops. I hold it before his nose. Ah, that still works. His tongue reaches out, gives a tentative taste. He licks his chops. Good, that, right, old boy? Right. I let him get another lick or two in before pulling the stick away. Now he's got some skin in the game, now it's worth the candle to play, innit? I cock the stick back and give my wrist a little flick. The stick goes two metres away. Fetch raises himself, goes over, and picks the stick up with his mouth. He trots back to his spot and settles in, licking the stick.

"There you are," I say. "He's still our Fetch." I look at Kissy as I say this. She shrugs, her mouth set in a line. Maybe she believes me, maybe not. Doesn't matter. At least she shut up about it.

"Whose turn is it to get a bottle?" Burke says.

"Mine." Randolph's hand is in the air.

Burke makes a sound of disgust. "A real bottle."

Randolph's face is screwed up, like he's ready to cry. He's getting red.

"I'll go," I say. "Randolph, you can come with me."

His face turns to instant glee, and he almost leaps up, spraying a bit of sand about.

"Hey, watch it," Wanda is not happy with being sprayed with sand. Good thing it wasn't Burke.

"Sorry," Randolph says.

Wanda mutters under her breath, but lets it go.

Randolph and I stand apart from the others.

"Which way shall we go today, Randolph?"

Randolph scrunches up his face, brows drawn together in a scowl as he looks down the beach one way, then turns and looks down the opposite way. He does this, back and forth, for several minutes.

"That way." He points.

"All right," I say. "That way it is." Doesn't really matter much. We've got caches up both directions. It'll be a good half hour before we get to the first one. Takes a real effort to go all the way and bring it back. Plus, it's so far you don't want to carry too much. By the time we finish the first go-round, nobody wants to make another trip. Thus, we don't just drink up the whole lot in one go. Smart of us, I think, to have come up with a system.

Randolph and I start walking. After a while we pass by the rusted metal hulk of some vehicle. Where were they trying to go? Did they just run out of land, driving until they came to the end?

We walk further, and see a freshie. I check his pockets as a matter of course, but he's got naught at all. I stand up, estimating how far away we are.

"We gonna cover him?" Randolph asks.

116

"Nah. No need. Not close enough for us to worry about."

"What if he gets cold?"

I look at Randolph. He seems concerned. I sigh. "Alright, let's do it."

He smiles at me and kneels with me in the sand to scoop handfuls over the freshie. We don't do a very good job of it, as my heart's not in it, but it's something.

"How's that?" I say.

"Good. He won't be cold now."

"Okay. Let's get going."

We walk some more. A long way. It's not like we have much else to do. Besides, they're probably bickering back at camp. That's about all we have left.

I see something in the sand up ahead. Sometimes things wash up. Once in a while, it's something fun. This isn't. It's a doll. I look at it for a minute, and turn away. Randolph looks at me.

"Aren't we going to take it?"

"No."

"But someone might be looking for it."

"Not anymore."

"You're crying. Are you crying for the doll?"

"No. The doll makes me sad, Randolph. Let's leave it."

He searches my face for the truth. The truth is, I don't like to be reminded. Dolls in particular are a reminder for me. I start walking. Randolph comes with me, but he keeps turning his head to watch the doll, as if he expected some little girl to come and get it. Soon enough, though, it's out of sight, and he seems to forget about it. He'll probably see it on the way back, though.

I wonder if we can stay out until after dark. That way we won't have to see it again.

We walk and we walk. I don't mind. Randolph is usually quiet, and it's nice without all the squabbling. Everything around us is dull gray. Everything.

After a long time, we come to a flag stuck upright in the sand. We kneel and dig until we uncover our stash. I take out four bottles, a few of the bags, and a few handfuls of pills. That should be enough for tonight. Don't want to overdo it. We lost Creech one night when we overdid it. Burke had brought back too much, and Creech just couldn't stop. Did he know what would happen? Who's to say? And who's to say he's worse off?

I hand two of the bottles to Randolph, and carry the rest myself. "Don't drop them," I say.

Looking very serious, he says "I'll be careful." And he will. He hasn't dropped one in a very long time. Burke beat him that time, maybe he remembers that.

I take two of the little white pills. Might as well get started. It's going to be a long night. Don't want to remember any more.

The pills help, and we eventually get back to the others.

"Where the fook have you been?" Burke is almost snarling. I hand him a bottle, and he snatches it from my hand.

"We found a freshie. We covered him up." I pass out the rest of the goodies, and the party begins. Drink, my friends, the water of Nepenthe. I lay back down, tired from our excursion. With two more pills, I swim away from the now.

I awake in the now, but it's always the now. Kissy is beside me, but I don't remember her coming to lay down with me. No one else seems awake. Everything isn't even gray yet, so the sun must not be up.

I get up and go down the beach to piss, letting my stream blend with the water. Then I sit and look out over the water, until I think I must resemble Smiley. I wonder what goes on in his head.

I get up and go back to the others, but everyone is still sleeping. Would I be doing them all a favor if I killed them in their sleep? So they wouldn't have to wake and find themselves back in the After, with another long day of nothing ahead? That could be the greatest mercy of all. But I don't. Maybe I'm a coward.

I slip in beside Kissy, and she stirs, and worms closer to me for warmth. It's good, and I feel myself stirring. One last reason to stay alive, maybe. I put an arm over her, and try to fall back asleep.

Sometime later, I wake up to the sound of someone yelling.

"Fetch! Fetch! Oh, I told you he was sick."

Kissy is on her knees beside Fetch, wailing. She pounds the sand with one fist.

"Stop that goddam keening, bitch," Burke groans.

I kneel beside Kissy. Fetch's one good eye is closed. I touch his fur, shake him at the shoulder. He doesn't move. I peel back the eyelid on the single eye, and flick a few grains of sand onto the eyeball. No movement. Gently, I lower the eyelid. Kissy is blubbering, almost hysterical. I put my arms around her.

Randolph is standing there, tears in his eyes. "He's gonna be alright, isn't he?"

I shake my head. "No Randolph, Fetch is gone."

"I told you he was sick," Kissy sobbed. She buries her head in my shoulder.

"Gonna miss him," says Wanda.

"I'm not," says Burke. "Foockin' hound."

"Shut up, you just shut up." Kissy is screaming now.

"You don't talk to me like that, girlie," Burke says. His voice drips with danger.

"Burke," I say. "Fetch is gone. He meant a lot to us, if not to you. Just this once, don't."

He looks at me with a dark glare, but only mutters under his breath.

Randolph is crying, Kissy is keeping up a kind of keening wail, Wanda has some tears splashing down, and my eyes are a little wet as well. Smiley says nothing, just keeps staring out to sea.

Long after everyone had cried themselves out, I picked up Fetch and took him a long, long way down the beach. I scooped out a hole in the sand and put him in, then covered him all over with more sand. It was more than many got, these nows.

Ruined buildings lay slanting and crumbled along the shore. So I went exploring. Never know what you might find. I looked through structures with walls and roofs shredded to ribbons, now exposing their guts to the elements.

My search turned up a child's red cowboy hat. I looked at it for a while, so incongruous here, in the now. The doll had a different meaning, a chain of rememberings from the Before. I couldn't face that, but this silly little hat had no rememberings in it. I thought Randolph might like it, so I picked it up and took it with me.

Building after building yielded nothing, all picked clean long ago. But I searched through all, just to be thorough.

And then I saw her.

She was huddled on the flat part of a collapsed veranda, staring out at the grayness of sea and sky. From a short distance, I halloed to her. She started, eyes wide, mouth open. She scrabbled away, as if I was a threat of some kind. Peering over the half-rail, she watched me, as if she would bolt if I got any closer. Probably scared of what I might do.

I took out the cowboy hat, put it on, and danced a little jig. I stopped and smiled, knowing I looked bloody ridiculous. She stared at me like I was a nutter, and then she laughed. It escaped, and she clamped a hand over her mouth.

"How do you do?" I called out. "Are you hungry? I have some food." I took off the hat and took out one of the old ration bars. I unwrapped a little bit of it slowly, showed it to her, and took a bite.

"Mmmm," I said, rubbing my belly. I tossed the bar over to her and smiled.

She looked down at it, then up at me.

"Go ahead, if you're hungry." I sat down to show I wasn't a threat.

It took a bit, but she eventually picked it up, and tried a tentative bite. She chewed slowly, but her face began to look interested. She gobbled the rest of it rather more quickly.

I held up my hands. "That's all I have right now. But there's more back with the others. Do you want to come?"

She looked at me as if she didn't understand what I said. Didn't know if she was head-hurt, or just didn't speak the lingo.

"Come with me," I said. "Back to our camp."

I held up my palm and walked two fingers across it, then pointed at her, and then at me. Then I pointed back the way I'd come. She cocked her head.

I beckoned her to come with me. She didn't move. I took a few steps away, and beckoned again, waiting. Her mouth bunched up, and I thought she was deciding. The she looked at me and made a brushing motion with her hand. Did she want me to leave? Oh well. I shrugged and started walking away. She came out from behind the rail, but when I stopped, she made the brushing motion again. I assumed it meant she wanted me to keep walking, and I was right. She'd follow me, but at a distance. Prudent lady, that.

So we walked, her about thirty paces behind me, watching me the whole time. She kept up well enough, but never got any closer. I strolled along, wondering what the others would say. We'd been together as our little group for so long, couldn't remember when the last newie came in.

We walked and walked, and I realized how far I'd gone. The grayness of the afternoon was getting darker, and I realized I might as well bring the party in when I came back. I doubted any of the others would have gone out for supplies. It always seemed to be me these days. So I looked for flags stuck in the sand and stopped at one of the small caches. She watched me dig, and I brought out four bottles, and one little bag. I popped a small green pill, stood and brushed the sand from me. I picked up the bottles and started walking. When I was far enough away, she followed.

It was dark by the time we got back, and they had a fire going. Most were eating. I came in and set down my load.

"Gone long enough," Burke said, crawling out just far enough to snag a bottle before crawling back into his shelter.

"We have a visitor," I said.

"What?" Wanda looked past me and gasped.

There was a commotion. Yeah, that got them up, didn't it? Everyone was talking at once.

I spoke to answer the question. "Found her by the old buildings. Don't know her name, or even if she understands me. Randolph, pass me that tin. I think she's hungry."

I turned and beckoned the woman forth. I held up the tin, opened it, and made eating motions, and rubbed my belly and smiled. Then I held the tin out to her.

Everyone was quiet now. She came slowly, hesitantly, looking at our faces. She took the tin from my hand, sniffed at the contents, and took a bite. She started eating, watching us all the while.

"Alright, let's go sit down. She can join us when she's ready."

"Where's she from?" Kissy was looking at the woman like she expected her to bite or pull a weapon.

"I told you, I don't know. She hasn't spoken yet."

"Well, where's she gonna sleep?"

I looked around. I hadn't thought of that.

"She can kip with me," Burke said, grinning. His teeth looked predatory in his face. Wanda's face grew red as her brows knit together, so I knew a storm was coming. If I'd have made a similar offer, Kissy would have done the same.

"I've got an extra tarp. We can make another shelter."

"Lot of bloody work, if you ask me," Burke said.

"I didn't. And what else have we got to do?"

"Fookin' drink," Burke said, talking a huge swallow.

I managed to get a makeshift shelter up, with no one else helping me. It wouldn't stay, but I could do better in the morning. I looked at the woman and pointed to the shelter, then to her. I put my hands together and held them against the side of my head and closed my eyes. I pointed at her again, and back at the shelter. She nodded.

The others were muttering, but they had their bottles and pills and smoke, and so left it alone. I took a swallow from a bottle and walked over to offer it to the woman. She shook her head. I shrugged and went back to my shelter and watched the fire for a while.

Kissy came to me a bit later and settled in beside me.

"I don't trust her," she said. 'We don't even know what to call her. And she doesn't talk."

"Smiley doesn't talk, either," I replied. "But she's one of us now, just like him."

"She is not one of us," I heard her hiss under her breath.

I awoke to the sound of wailing. Wanda was staggering around, crying and sobbing.

"He's dead. He's dead. Oh God, no."

"Burke?" I said. Truth be told, if it was any of us, I'd prefer it to be him.

"Smiley!" she cried out, her arm dramatically pointing to his tired little shelter.

I got up and went to see. Smiley lay in the sand, unmoving. I squatted down and put my fingers to the side of his neck. I felt nothing, and his skin was cold. I saw a broken piece of mirror in amongst Smiley's few pitiful belongings, and I reached for it. I held the surface of the shard close to Smiley's mouth and nose, but there was no vapor. He was gone.

I stood up. The others were looking at me. I shook my head. Wanda began to cry again. Kissy stood with her arms crossed.

"She killed him."

"What?" I looked at her. She pointed to the new woman. "Her. She must have killed him. Smiley was fine yesterday, but you brought her here, and now he's dead."

"Don't be stupid. Her being here had nothing to do with Smiley's death."

"How do you know she didn't kill him?"

"How do we know YOU didn't kill him, my dear?" Burke leered at her.

Kissy looked at him, her lips set in a tight line. She looked like she wanted to say something nasty, but it was Burke, and she held it in.

"Send her away," Kissy said. She doesn't belong here."

"She has nowhere else to go. No one does. Anyone that's left belongs with us."

Kissy turned away.

"We were fine until she came. No one died."

"Fetch died," said Randolph. We all looked at him. He hung his head. "Maybe it was Smiley's turn."

No one spoke for a while. Kissy saw she wasn't going to get her way. "You can't leave him here."

I looked at her. I was getting bloody tired of doing all the work. "Randolph, would you help me please? We're going to take Smiley down the beach aways."

"Like we did with Fetch?" Randolph's face was all screwed up. I didn't want to take him, but I felt worn out. I needed his help. I nodded.

I didn't think we could carry Smiley far enough, so we took the few things out of his shelter and took him out on his tarp. With Randolph and I dragging one edge, we were able to slide him along the sand.

It was a lot of work. We stopped to rest often. I looked at the poor bugger lying there, and wondered when his last real thought was, and what had kept him going after that. I realized I didn't want to think about that any more.

After a very long time, I felt we had come far enough. Randolph and I started to dig. That was more work, and we had to rest quite a bit. Finally we wrapped Smiley in his tarp and got him in the depression we had made for him. A house of sand. We scooped more sand all over, until he was properly covered. We did a better job than we had for the freshie. Smiley was one of us.

We sat breathing heavily when we had finished. Randolph looked at me.

"Am I gonna die, too? Like Fetch and Smiley? So you'll cover me with sand?"

"Oh no, Randolph. We're going to be around for a very long time."

"Oh."

I thought he'd be happier to hear that. But it seemed to depress him even more. I didn't know what to say, because I was afraid he'd start a crying jag. I felt rather near to one myself.

We began the long walk back. I looked at the grayness in the distance. It was hard to tell where the sky ended and the sea began. It was almost all one. I felt a great sadness come over me.

I took my time getting back to the others. No one said anything when Randolph and I got back. There was a silence, a watchfulness as we came in to the camp. I looked around. The new woman was gone.

"Where is she?" I was speaking to them all. No one spoke. Kissy was standing with her arms crossed, a strange look on her face. I walked over to her and took her and grabbed her upper arms.

"Where is she?" I almost shouted it.

"She left."

"Left? You mean you drove her out."

"No. She knew she didn't belong, and left."

I looked at Wanda, who would not meet my gaze. I looked at Burke, whose eyes shone with a strange light. Then I knew.

I slapped Kissy hard across the face. Her mouth was open in shock, her hand touching where I'd struck, like she'd been burned.

"Where?"

She shrugged. I wanted to slap her again, but realized it was no use.

I looked around, and saw where the sand had been smoothed over somewhat, leading out of camp. They had dragged her out, and then tried to cover it, but it was poorly done, because they were lazy and sloppy. It was easy to see where they had gone. They hadn't gone very far, barely out of sight of camp. I saw where the sand had been disturbed. They hadn't covered enough of her, and I scooped sand away to see.

The back of her head was bloody, the skull smashed in. I touched her lightly, my hand on her shoulder.

"I'm sorry."

I spent some time heaping new sand on her, until she was covered properly. I stood and looked back at camp. I didn't want to go back there just yet. I didn't know what I would do. I walked down the beach, away from the others. I walked a long time.

At one point, I passed a flag sticking up out of the sand. I nodded, as if I'd received a signal of some kind. I dug until I found a bottle, took it out, opened it, and began drinking.

It was some time later I noticed the bottle was gone. The grayness was edging toward dark. I looked around, and felt the cold of Ruination Beach, what we'd named the place when we first came here. We'd wandered until we could go no more, and then just planted ourselves.

For what purpose, I wondered. Spinning out our remaining days arguing and drinking, dying off one by one. There was no more purpose in the After, no point in the now. It was done.

I dug more bottles out of the sand. Five more, one for each of us left. I took out two bags, and removed some of the small yellow pills. They helped us sleep without nightmares, when we needed it. I opened four of the bottles and poured in a half-dozen of the yellow pills into each bottle and resealed them. I put the bags in my pocket, stood up, and gathered the bottles.

I walked back to camp in the dark. I saw the fire from a long way off, one pitiful beacon in the blackness surrounding us. At least they could still do that.

When I came into camp, they watched me closely, as if wondering what I would do. I deliberately put a bottle in front of each person, and dropped the bags by the fire. They smiled, assuming it was an offering, that everything was alright. I went to my shelter without speaking to anyone, and began to drink some more. Mine was the unopened bottle, at least until now. They started their party.

Things had changed. Later in the night, Kissy went to Burke's shelter, and Wanda lay apart, crying loudly until Burke snarled at her to shut up. I knew what had caused the change. It didn't matter, it only confirmed what needed to be done. I lay awake, not drinking after a while, feeling sick. I hadn't eaten, but I couldn't now. Now with what had to be done.

I got up in the dark, the fire low and almost burned out. I took the center pole from my shelter, a stout wooden thing shorter than me. I walked over to Burke's shelter, where he and Kissy were snoring quite loudly. There were tears in my eyes as I lifted the pole over my head and brought it down on Burke's. There was a sickly, plopping sound. It had done for him, sure enough. Kissy did not stir, but continued to snore. I lifted the pole again and did her the same mercy.

Poor outcast Wanda was next, gone without a whimper, or a bang, as it were. The only one I hesitated with was Randolph. He lay clutching the red cowboy hat I'd brought him, his little treasure. Poor fool, like Lear's Cordelia, a simple, innocent man. But in the end, he would suffer no more.

It was just me now. I took up my bottle that had plenty left in it, and dumped the remaining pills into it, shaking the bottle to dissolve them. More than enough. I would drink, and sleep, and never wake up. Farewell to Ruination Beach, farewell to a world so stupid that it couldn't save itself from itself.

The fire was gone, and darkness closed in around me.

Dale T. Phillips

OUR LADY

Something was very wrong, Pepe knew. It was only a few days until Christmas, and he thought that everyone should be happy, but the grownups were arguing and crying instead, even the men, and no one would tell him why. After the fighting and crying, the grownups would be quiet for a time, the silence broken only by the constant wail of sirens from the outside world, and the sound of gunshots that increased as the day went on.

The apartment was overflowing with family and a few friends, most of them watching the television set that had been on all day. Pepe wanted the grownups to work on getting ready for Christmas, not watching television, but they brusquely shooed him away if he tried to talk to them.

Men on the flickering screen were talking about something called a deadline, and missiles, and the grownups would comment in loud voices after each man spoke.

"We should try to go somewhere," said Mr. Hernandez, who lived two doors down. "Get out of the city, at least."

"Where?" The reply was sharp, and came from Pepe's cousin Miguel. "It's the whole world. There's no place to go. And we couldn't anyway. The roads are all jammed."

"Maybe they won't do it. They'll come to their senses, won't they?"

"They did fifty years ago," said Carlos, who was very old. His voice was papery and thin. "It was over Cuba. They came close, but they stopped. They won't do it this time either."

Several people spoke at once, and it was all a jumble of voices again.

Pepe was getting bored, because he couldn't understand many of the words the television men were saying. He was also a little hungry. Though many people in the barrio were very poor, Pepe's family usually had more than enough to eat, especially on holidays, when the grownups got together. But it seemed no one was interested in eating; instead they just sat and watched the television, and talked about what it all meant.

Pepe did not know who to speak to about getting some food. Pepe's father, in his chair in front of the television, was drinking heavily, as were many others. Mama had retreated to her bedroom with the door closed, praying to her shrine of Santa Maria. Pepe went down the hall to his room, and saw his cousin Maurice come out of the bathroom.

"Are you okay?" Pepe looked at the much older boy. "Your eyes are red."

Maurice ran his sleeve over his eyes. "I'm gonna be fine soon enough."

"Why?"

"I've always wanted a motorcycle. So I'm gonna go get one."

"For Christmas?"

Maurice looked startled, then the ghost of a smile played over his face. "Yeah. My Christmas present, to me."

"Where'd you get the money?"

"No money. I'm gonna go steal one."

"But won't you go to jail?"

"Ain't nobody going to jail anymore, little man."

"How come?"

"There's better things to do on your last night."

"Last night of what?"

"Last night of life. See ya around, kid."

Maurice walked away, and Pepe frowned. This was very strange. He went back to his bedroom and thought for a long time.

When he emerged from his room at last, his favorite tio was coming down the hall, and Pepe ran to him, throwing his arms around the man's legs. "Uncle Rafael!"

"Hello, there. Let me get a look at you."

Pepe looked up into his uncle's face. "Have you been crying, too?"

"Yes, Pepe."

"Why is everyone crying? Is it the things the men on the television are saying?"

His uncle looked back, as if searching for something. "Yes."

"Is it something to do with Christmas?"

His uncle looked at him strangely, and then shook his head. "No, I wish it was just that."

"So we'll still have Christmas?"

His uncle ruffled Pepe's hair. "If you could have anything in the world for a present, what would you want?"

"A bicycle," Pepe answered quickly. "Papa says we don't have the money, but I want one more than anything."

His uncle wiped his eye with the back of a hand. "And if you had a bicycle, what color would it be?"

"Red!"

"Red," said his uncle.

"Why is Mama in her room?"

"She's praying to Our Lady. She thinks if she prays hard enough, maybe this thing won't happen."

"What thing?"

His uncle pursed his lips, then put on a smile. "Did you know this city is named for Our Lady?"

"It is?"

"Yes. It's really called *Nuestra Señora la Reina de los Angeles*, Our Lady the Queen of the Angels, but we just say the last part."

"Mama says Our Lady watches over us all the time. Like Santa."

"Santa and Santa Maria. Very clever. You know the difference, don't you, Pepe?"

"I think so. But they're both kind, and watch over us, and want us to do good things."

"Yes, they do." Rafael looked around. "Pepe, maybe you should go back to your room now. I'll come by a little later, alright?"

"Okay."

Pepe went to his room, and soon realized he had forgotten to ask Uncle Rafael about getting some food. His stomach rumbled with all kinds of interesting noises. He could hear other noises, too, like his sisters arguing in the next room, though they had not raised their voices. It was just that the walls were so thin.

"I don't care. I'm going to do it. I'm going to his place and do it," said Juanita.

"You can't. It's a sin," he heard Carmen say.

"I don't care," replied Juanita. "If we're going to die, I don't want to die a virgin."

Pepe knew virgins had something to do with Our Lady, but what did his sister mean? He hoped that as he got older, he would finally understand what people were talking about.

Pepe surrendered to his growling stomach. He padded out to the living room, but all the grownups still seemed hypnotized by the men talking on the television. He went to the empty kitchen and got a chair to stand on to reach a bowl in the cupboard. He took out a box of cereal, and shook some into the bowl. He got the milk from the refrigerator and poured it over the cereal, but some sloshed out onto the table. He darted a guilty glance at the other room, but no one had seen him spill. He took the old dish towel and carefully wiped up the mess. Then he sat at the table by himself, crunching slowly.

When he had finished, he put his empty bowl in the sink, and once more stood at the back of the living room and watched all the grownups with their faces turned to the television. He shook his head and went back to his room to play. He took out a coloring book filled with dinosaurs that his tio had got for him at a thrift store, and the four short crayons. For inspiration, he looked at his favorite toy, a red plastic T. Rex with one foot missing.

Pepe colored for a while until he was drowsy, and napped on the floor of his room. There was a knock, and Uncle Rafael was in the bedroom doorway.

"Your face is bleeding, tio," Pepe said.

"It's nothing," Rafael said. "Pepe, come out in the hall. I have a surprise for you."

Pepe did as he had been asked, and went out to see a new bicycle leaning against the wall.

"It's for you," Rafael said. "Merry Christmas, Pepe."

Pepe gasped. "It's beautiful. And red, just like I wanted."

"You like it?"

"It's the best present ever," Pepe replied. "I want to ride it. Can we go outside so I can ride?"

His uncle made a strange face, as if he'd seen something scary. "No, Pepe, it's not safe outside right now. We'll go ride tomorrow, okay?"

Pepe ran his hands over every surface of the bike, feeling the tires, the seat, the frame, the toothed gears, the metal handlebars. It was like a dream, and all the grownup strangeness he'd been worrying about melted away. He looked back at his uncle, whose eyes were wet.

"Uncle, are you crying again?"

"I'm just happy you like the bike."

"I love it. And I love you, tio. Thank you so much."

"I love you too, Pepe."

Pepe frowned. "We didn't wait for Christmas, though. Is that bad?"

"No, it's okay. Christmas is just early this year."

"Santa won't be mad?"

His uncle coughed. "Santa will understand. He'll be happy that you're happy."

"I am. I wish everyone could be, though. Everyone seems so sad. What's going on?"

His uncle rubbed a palm over his face, and looked at the bit of blood that stained his hand. "People are fighting, Pepe. They've gone crazy, and are going to war."

"How could they fight, with Christmas coming up? Don't they know Santa's watching?"

"They don't care. They just want to hurt each other."

"They won't hurt us, though, will they?"

His uncle squatted down and put his unbloodied hand on Pepe's shoulder. "No, they won't hurt us. You just enjoy your bike. I'm going to sit with your papa and the others. Let's get the bike into your room."

His uncle wheeled the cycle into the bedroom and left. With the bike in the room, there was almost no space to move around in, but Pepe didn't care. He kept touching the bike, unable to believe he owned something so magical. He counted the spokes, and read all the lettering on every surface. He noticed a small smear of blood on the frame, and wiped it off with a dirty sock. He used a dark one so mama wouldn't see and be angry at him.

The bike kept him busy for a long time. But he felt lonely, and went out to the living room. The grownups all looked at the screen, where a man with a microphone was speaking.

Other than the talking man, everything was silent. Pepe slipped onto Rafael's lap, as tears ran down the older man's face. His tio hugged Pepe tightly, so tightly that it hurt, but Pepe didn't move or talk.

Someone spoke. "Nothing. Feel it? They didn't do it," and a ragged cheer arose, amid sobs of relief.

Then the rumble began, shaking the building, and there were screams.

Pepe squirmed free, and ran to the window as the apartment shook. He looked out over the city, into the sky lit with bright fire. As he stared into the flames, he thought he saw Our Lady herself. She was very beautiful, Pepe admitted, even as she wept and looked down over her city, and her world, full of burning angels.

YOUR OPINION MATTERS!

If you liked this book, please consider leaving a review on any of the sites:
Amazon, Goodreads, Barnes and Noble.

Good reviews help others to find quality books to read, and greatly help the author to reach a broader audience.

Thank you in advance.

Acknowledgments

My thanks extend to everyone who helped to make this book possible.

As always, to my wonderful family: Mindy, Bridget, and Erin, for suffering my otherwise solitary profession of writing.

To my dear and supportive friends for making things more enjoyable along the path of life.

To all those who have helped teach me to write, through their works.

To all those who read other works of mine and wanted more.

And to you, dear reader, my thanks, for reading this one.

Feel free to contact me and let me know what you thought of the book and what it's about.

Afterword

As you read some of these stories, you'll notice a recurrent theme in a few of them-- The Question-- how to go on living when we have lost the one we love, and the pain is too great to bear. Too many people in this world have dealt with such suffering, and some have chosen not to continue life in so much pain. Some of these tales offer a redemption, a last chance to consider before taking that drastic step.

Another story considers what we are as a race, what choices lie ahead, and what might have helped get us here. By journeying into our past, sometimes we can see our future. The future is not predetermined-- we will make of it what we will. Whether or not we will finish ourselves off is a matter yet to be seen. But we've had the capacity to end all life on the planet for 80 years, and we haven't done so yet, so there's hope.

Another story is a complete changeup, for we shouldn't be grim all the time. Here we play with language in the manner of Lewis Carroll or James Joyce, with puns and portmanteau words galore.

Anyway, enjoy the ride. The stories await....

**

About the Author

A lifelong student of mysteries, Maine, and more, the travels and background of Dale T. Phillips allow him to draw upon a colorful life to portray troubled people coping with dangerous situations.

Dale studied writing with Stephen King, and has published novels, collections, poetry, articles, non-fiction, and over 80 short stories. He has appeared on stage, television, and in an independent feature film. He has also appeared on *Jeopardy*, losing in a spectacular fashion. He co-wrote and acted in a short political satire film.

He has traveled to all 50 states, Mexico, Canada, and through Europe.

Connect Online:
Website: http://www.daletphillips.com
Blog: http://daletphillips.blogspot.com

***

Try these other works by Dale T. Phillips

Shadow of the Wendigo (Supernatural Thriller)
Neptune City (Mystery)
Locust Time (Suspense)
Desert Heat (Crime/Mystery)

The Zack Taylor Mystery Series

A Great Reckoning
A Darkened Room
A Sharp Medicine
A Certain Slant of Light
A Shadow on the Wall
A Fall From Grace
A Memory of Grief

Dale T. Phillips

Story Collections

The Big Book of Genre Stories (Different Genres)
Crime Time (Mystery/Crime)
Halls of Fear (Horror)
Journeys and Ends (Magic Realism, End of the World)
All the Crooked Paths (Mystery/Crime)
All the Fables and Fantasies (Fantasy)
Jumble Sale (Different Genres)

Non-fiction Career Help

How to be a Successful Indie Writer
87 Ways to Sell More Books
How to Conquer Excuses and Just Write
How to Win
How to Improve Your Interviewing Skills

Sign up for my newsletter to get special offers
http://www.daletphillips.com

Made in United States
North Haven, CT
13 September 2025

72588645R00078